DEATH LIVES ON SKI MOUNTAIN...

"Get me off!" screamed Janice Pace, Miss Great Northern Resort's Snow Queen of 1977, as the chairlift passed the booth on the advanced slope. Suddenly she saw reaching toward her a grotesquely clawed hand. She swerved away, crashing into the metal pole dividing the lift.

The fingers groped, and the form pursued her, keeping pace with the lift.

The fingers were upon her, touching her, squeezing the bone in her arm; she felt it splinter.

A low agonized whine was the only sound she was capable of.

SNOWMAN

Norman Bogner

A DELL BOOK

Published by
Dell Publishing Co., Inc.
1 Dag Hammarskjold Plaza
New York, New York 10017

Dell ® TM 681510, Dell Publishing Co., Inc.

ISBN: 0-440-18152-6

Printed in the United States of America

First printing—February 1978

For Robby Wald
and Bob Eisenstein
for the pleasure
of their friendship.

In 1966, five years after the Edmund Hillary Expedition to Mount Everest, another group, known as "The Bradford Search," was stopped at the Lhotse Face. They were then at an altitude of 27,980 feet, three miles south of the summit of Everest, separated from it by the South Col and a long ridge over 25,000 feet high. Except for Bradford and his Sherpa guide, Pemba, the entire party mysteriously disappeared, in circumstances that have never been explained.

Prologue

Along the wall of the Lhotse Face the towers of ice rose like twisted needles as the endless night slowly dissolved into an explosion of fierce sunlight which blinded Bradford. He and Pemba lay motionless on a pitch of ice, though they both knew they had to move or freeze.

Frenzied animals slithered down the glacier. Snow leopards, wild yaks, and the great black-faced monkeys known as langurs plunged to their death just above him. The Lhotse Face, littered with bodies and carcasses, had become a slaughterhouse. Bradford and his team—and now the animals—were being purged from the mountain.

The signs of the rampage were everywhere. Packs of tailless Tibetan rats scurried down crevasses. Musk deer which had wandered away from their herds lay decapitated in stinking blood-soaked piles. Crisscrossing the climbing trail were monstrously large triangular rainbow-colored tracks.

It had been impossible to foresee that Bradford's

9

search for the Snowman would terminate in this devastating spectacle. Based on all the sightings and reports Bradford had read about, he had hoped to locate a mammal of some kind, covered with reddish hair, and no larger than a man—a rogue strain of the ape family which had adapted to a glacial environment. From his early student days in anthropology, Bradford had theorized that such a creature could exist in these climatic conditions, even though his colleagues at Harvard had scoffed at the notion. Only field work, he had felt, outside the confines of a university hothouse, could prove his case.

He had been wrong on all counts. The Snowman was something else, beyond classification, a mutant which had been formed in a prehistoric age. As a result of Bradford's quest, ten sherpa porters and nine men in his party were already dead—hacked to death, their dismembered bodies consumed by a beast with an insatiable hunger for human flesh.

Now Bradford was in flight with Pemba, the only Sherpa guide still alive. They slithered across the ice, stumbling on their broken crampons, driven by the stark terror of being eaten.

The sixty-mile-an-hour wind became a bellows as it channeled between towering pinnacles of ice and the great saddle of the South Col. But there was another sound, playing a violent counterpoint with the wind, frightening enough to drive the men onward—a piercing hum that came through the rarefied air. As they pushed ahead, the mountain seemed to be collapsing; the surface of the glacier split and twisted into a maze of chasms. The two men staggered onto a ledge.

It was hopeless, Bradford sensed, even as he and Pemba went through the motions of tying the nylon rope around their waists in a bowline. Bradford could hardly bend his fingers. He had lost his windproof woolen gloves and was now down to the last layers, which were made of silk; his caked blood stuck to them, making it agonizing to hold the rope.

Pemba slashed the ice with his ax, digging in up to the haft.

Bradford reeled giddily, but the sensation lasted only for an instant. Just above him, blending in with the tortured ridges of the sérac he had moved from, was a pair of eyes, hollow caverns the size of saucers. They had no irises, and the beams of light they emitted revealed impenetrable depths. Bradford stood hypnotized as Pemba pleaded with him from below to climb down. The light from the eyes was melting the snow, creating a throbbing cataract of hissing water.

A gigantic arm reached out for him. The skin was gray, leatherish, armored with sharp bonelike protuberances. The Snowman moved in an upright position, and Bradford was paralyzed by the colossal size of him. He must have been over twenty feet tall. Pemba pulled on the rope to signal Bradford, but his voice was lost in the violent reverberations of the Snowman's roar. From the creature's gnarled fingers retractable claws the size of butcher knives flicked out. Bradford felt the flesh being torn from his shoulder blade. A mouth, a black orifice with rows of swordlike teeth, opened wide as Bradford lurched back. Pemba was climbing toward him, shrieking in Nepalese to divert attention away from Bradford. But the Snowman was closing in on Bradford. His massive horned feet crunched on the slope, and fragments of ice filled the air.

The platform of the ice step collapsed, but Bradford had only a dim realization of falling. He was weightless, his arms and legs tangled in the guy ropes like a marionette's. His fall was broken by a mound of soft, powdery snow.

Human hands seized him and pulled him into a cave, where there was firelight. The smell inside was putrid, and he watched through glazed, disbelieving eyes as robed men struggled with a large boulder and rolled it to the mouth of the ice cave, blocking out the tormented cries of the stampeding, hysterical animals.

Bradford heard only silence now, the sweet silence of the dark which had been denied him when the Snowman's claws had touched him. No more could he await the release of immediate death. He felt pain, he was still matter, he could think: He was terrified.

The cakes of ice these men were laying on his wound numbed his flesh. In the glow of the fire at the rear of the cave he made out the spectral forms of men, and he knew who they were.

When the search had begun, his party had stopped at the Buddhist monastery of Thyangboche to pay respects to the abbot, and he had heard about the Tibetan lamas who lived high on Everest, men who dedicated their lives to placating the Snowman, whom they called the Yeti. They believed that their presence prevented the Yeti from destroying the Sherpa villages at the foot of the mountain. He had asked Pemba, his head guide and the *sirdar* or manager of the Sherpa porters, about them, but Pemba had refused to confirm or deny the existence of the sect. His reaction was typical, a refusal to discuss religious matters, for a vein of profound and unshakable mysticism ran through these Sherpa tribesmen.

But the evidence was before Bradford. Through the sealed cave he heard the spitting of a giant cat, which caused him to shudder. From the reaction of the men in the cave, he knew that the Snowman was just outside. The Snowman's ability to mimic other animals was part of the legend, a way of concealing and camouflaging his movements.

As the roars—now those of a mountain lion—grew louder, Bradford wondered if he wouldn't have preferred to die alone on the mountain, in mortal combat with the Yeti, rather than suffocating in a cave filled with these doomed holy lamas, who could accept death passively, according to some Oriental idea which he could never understand.

He craned his neck, searching for Pemba; then it occurred to him that Pemba might still be outside . . . A procession of lamas approached him with flickering torches. They were wearing hideous painted devil masks and swaying in a serpentine Lamaist ceremonial dance. Some held prayer wheels; others blew conch shells. In the rear of the cave, sitting by the fire, were two lamas sounding the great Tibetan ceremonial horns, some fourteen feet in length. The charivari of these sounds mixing with the droning chants disturbed him. He shifted his weight and struggled to his knees.

The lamas were before him now, and he could see that all of them had been horribly mutilated in some way. Several were blind, with livid scars across their faces; others had lost arms and legs. Maimed, mauled, and mangled by whom? he asked himself.

In a jumble of words, some Nepalese and Mongolian, he heard the answers:

"*Meh-Teh!*" a lama shouted, kneeling on one leg.

A manlike thing that is not human.

"Dzu-Teh!" an armless Lama shrieked at the boulder. A hulking thing.

Behind them, being carried on a filthy litter made of reindeer skins, a mockery of a throne, was a creature with Oriental features slicked by the fat of ram chikor. All that remained of this being was a torso, covered in an abbot's red prayer shawl, a scarf draped across the wrinkled neck. The creature was lifted from the litter and brought closer to him. The abbot's eyes were two gray filmy cataracts. It was a vision straight from hell.

Beside the abbot stood Pemba, his palms together, his fingers extended upward. Bradford feebly touched his guide's shoes in a gesture of gratitude. The abbot's tongue was guided to Bradford's wound. Bradford squirmed as the tongue licked his raw, torn flesh. The contact sickened him, and for a moment he thought that the ritual was a form of farewell before he was to be offered to the Yeti as a sacrifice.

The procession passed him and moved to the mouth of the cave. Bradford crawled away toward the deserted fire. The lamas laid holy red Khadas at the foot of the boulder and spun prayer wheels. They then formed a circle around the abbot's litter and joined hands. In a trancelike dance, they undulated and chanted their mystical holy prayer over and over again in a low, sepulchral chorus:

"Om Mane Padme Om . . ."

The jewel is in the lotus.

The repetition made his eyelids droop. He mustn't sleep. He lit an incense stick and staggered to his feet, lurching against the walls of the cave like a drunk.

"Om Mane Padme Om . . ."

On a flat smooth surface of the wall he saw cave paintings of the Yeti. Below the Yeti was the miniature figure of an archer with an arrow poised in his bow.

The chanting stopped abruptly, and a thin reedy voice coming from the upraised litter cried:

"*Sogpa. Sogpa. Sogpa!*"

Bradford stretched out to brace himself, but he began falling, losing consciousness and entering a long black tunnel of dreamless sleep.

Chapter One

Beauty queens are a headache. Before their coronations they have a charming naive innocence that is consistent with the flaky mental process that enables them to enter such events. But afterward, the soft curves, the sweet little backside that jiggles on command on a stage, and the gaiety of the empty smile suddenly assume the rock-hardness of a frozen mountain cliff.

Janice Pace, Miss Great Northern Resort's Snow Queen of 1977, was no exception. She was demanding, peevish, a whiner of great distinction. It seemed only fitting and just that she should become Cathy Parker's problem. It was Cathy, Great Northern's public relations and advertising director, who had thought up the gimmick of a contest to endow the opening of the company's new ski resort in Sierra with the trappings of glamour.

Cathy was a tall, lithe woman with chestnut hair, which she wore shoulder length. Her eyes were hazel and contained an edge of worldly perceptiveness which had matured in the male society she moved in. She suffered from her own intelligence, for she had discovered that, far from regarding it an asset, the men she came in contact with felt threatened and inhibited, preferring to treat her as one of the boys rather than as a woman.

Great Northern's Lear jet had been delayed three hours, and Cathy's whole schedule had been thrown off. By the time the garishly painted orange creation with its logo of a pyramid containing the symbol of infinity finally set down at the Sierra airport, many members of the reception committee had left.

Of the original party, only a local hired photographer, along with Jim Ashby, editor-publisher-reporter of the *Sierra Messenger,* remained to welcome the Queen. The Sierra High School Band had gone off to rehearse their program for the school's Thanksgiving hockey game. Sierra's alderman had departed for a Lions' luncheon, where he was the keynote speaker. None of this, however, was as serious as the discipline situation Cathy faced with the Queen's retainers. The four ski instructors acting as the Queen's coachmen were decked out in outlandish Viking costumes with fur stoles and horned brass helmets, and by noon their mutiny had reached alarming proportions.

They had polished off two cases of Coors and were now smoking grass in the back of the old covered wagon that had been designated the Queen's coach. Cathy knew better than to threaten the boys, because it wasn't possible to find certified instructors at the beginning of the first holiday weekend.

When the plane taxied in, Janice was first off. She looked lumpy in a big brown parka.

"They sent the wrong size clothes," she complained. "Fourteens." Her attention wandered to the gold-painted coach and the banner draped across it. "Oh, terrific. They got my name wrong. It's Janice, not Janet."

"We've got one part-time signmaker in Sierra, but I'll see what I can do," Cathy said.

"What a mess," Janice protested.

"It's not that serious," Cathy said.

"Oh, I don't mean the damned sign. I've got an earache from the flight, I'm starved, and I'm late with my period."

Her retainers began a slow mocking charade of greeting her, which did little to restore the good humor that had characterized her personality on the nightclub stage in Los Angeles where she had won her title.

"Where'd these turkeys come from?" she said, loud enough to be heard by the Vikings. Cathy closed her eyes as though to avoid the sight of a car crash.

The instructors decided to ignore the remark. They kept the elegant cool which had made their astounding number of sexual conquests a source of envy to other men.

Cathy stationed Janice at the window of the coach, positioning her so the photographer could get some publicity shots.

The local news team arrived in a van and was induced to film the royal entourage on its journey up to the lodge. The persuasion took the form of a promise by Cathy to buy some more spots on the wilderness that was *Sierra Update,* a program largely given over to weather reports for hunters, skiing conditions, and interviews with colorful ice-fishing personalities in the area.

They got to film more than they had expected. While Cathy watched in horror from the company jeep, the instructors took their revenge on Janice by lashing the four drays into a frenzy, nearly overturning the wagon. Their passenger screamed helplessly from the back seat while she held on to the collapsing frame of the door.

On their arrival at the lodge, the driver held open the door for the Snow Queen and said:

"Welcome to the Mustang Ranch, sister."

Cathy pulled in between the factions and managed to restore order. By this time, the instructors were threatening to quit. Janice, with tears creating a bayou of mascara, was led through the lobby up to her suite overlooking Cobra, the advanced ski run. She shouted at the top of her voice:

"If there wasn't a twenty-five-hundred-dollar cash prize in this I'd go back to L.A. right this second."

In the executive offices, Monte Dale, the director responsible for the birth of the resort, "a Disneyland on snow," was listening intently and with a growing sense of anxiety to Cathy's account.

He was a small, ferrety man who watched his weight with the same attention he gave the company's money. Great Northern Resorts was his responsibility, and the twenty-five million dollars the company had shelled out on his say-so would make him unemployable if the ski resort turned out to be Death Valley.

"What do you mean, she can't ski?" He pointed an accusing finger at Cathy.

"Well, she lied. You were there at the Roxy when she was interviewed."

"She should have been disqualified if she can't ski."

"I know that."

"Cathy, with sixty contestants, how did we get this

lemon? Who *did* this to us?" Paranoia was finding a permanent residence in his tirades.

"There was no way of testing her in L.A. It was ninety-eight degrees and the girls were in bikinis."

"Get her ass on the slopes. She's going to be skiing by this afternoon. Tell Barry that I want him to teach her."

"Barry's out giving a downhill exhibition for the new arrivals."

"I don't give a damn."

"But Barry thinks of himself as a performer."

"That's the bottom line, Cathy," he said, dismissing her and glaring at the sales charts on his office wall. "Barry gets five hundred a week for two hours' work a day and all the foxes he can handle. This once he can make an exception and teach a yo-yo the fundamentals."

"Monte, she doesn't want to learn. She's afraid."

"I don't want to hear about it. Get them together."

Cathy waited at the bottom of the expert's slope for Barry Harkness, the resort's name downhill skier. He was a prima donna who had been recruited from Vail. Nominally in charge of the ski school, he did little but practice, though all his efforts hadn't qualified him for the U.S. Olympic team. An almost-ran with the temperament of a soprano, off the slopes he appeared at the resort's social functions and danced all night at the Snowplow Discothèque or stood being admired by a throng of women. But he was worth it to Great Northern. His name was plastered on all the ads the resort ran, because despite his Olympic failure, he was still a celebrity with skiers. Not many people can ski down a twelve-thousand-foot mountain at seventy miles an hour without crippling themselves.

An audience applauded his downhill run, and Barry greeted them with a wave of his poles and a fey smile. Janice and he would make a perfect couple, Cathy thought as she edged into the group of instructors. They'd produce large massive-boned Nordic children with straight teeth and ruddy skin, who were complete idiots.

Cathy took Barry aside, razzle-dazzled him with flattery, then laid her dilemma on him. She concluded by saying, "You've never seen anything like her—all woman, could be Farrah Fawcett-Major's twin sister."

He nodded approvingly. "Okay, she gets a lesson." Then, having second thoughts, he asked the instructors who had served in her retinue, "What's this muffin really like?"

"She's got a loose deck," said one.

"Love it," Barry replied, an uncomplicated emotion playing across his impassive face.

"She won't be easy," said another.

Cathy listened patiently to the macho, juvenile chatter, hoping the challenge would entice Barry.

"She'll be screaming by the time she's off the chairlift, and we'll be snowplowing by cocktail hour," Barry said confidently.

"Twenty dollars says you von't," said Erich, the Kitzbühel *Wunderkind*. He had been hired in spite of bad references (three paternity suits against him the previous season) when Monte had insisted on having somebody with a German accent, to lend European dignity to the instructional staff.

"My method never fails," Barry began expansively. He nodded to Cathy, treating her as one of the boys.

"Her arches and ankles will be aching. Muscles pulled in the calves. Her can'll be sore, and that's when, gentlemen, I'll recommend my St. Moritz special foot bath . . ."

"How's it work, Barry?" Cathy asked.

"I run a hot tub, add a jigger of rum, two of Lavoris, and a squeeze of Vitabath to make the water bubble. Muffin takes off her warm-ups, slips into a robe. Then I plant the flags for the Giant Slalom."

"If you skied like you pork you'd be an Olympic gold medalist," Baxter, a lean ex-Aspen skeptic, said.

"Barry, you can't make a conquest just talking. It's time you met Janice," Cathy said.

"You're on for twenty, Kraut," Barry said. "Anyone else?"

Chapter Two

In the timeless universe inhabited by the Snowman there was no sense of location. He had been formed in the graveyard of Antarctica just as the ice age, the Pleistocene Epoch, was ending and Neolithic man was beginning to evolve.

The extreme climatic changes which altered the land masses of what came to be known as Asia and the Americas forced the Snowman to adapt to his surroundings and gradually mutate.

As he grew larger, he fed on dying whales and sharks in the Antarctic, and when this source of life became scarce, he moved on. The hair on his body had become rock-hard bonelike extensions, and his gray skin had been able to absorb ice and fuse it so that it shielded him from the elements.

As his appetite increased, his digestive tract and biochemical glandular functions became more sophisticated. He had always been a flesh eater and through the ages had fed on the various species of man which had evolved. Java, Peking, and Heidelberg man lived in caves to protect themselves from the cold and from this enemy who preyed on them. But as temperatures became warmer and deserts formed, the Snowman was driven higher and higher into the Trans-Himalayan mountainous regions, where the volcanic activity had subsided. There he had an ample supply of animals, which he stalked relentlessly, until they too began to disappear.

The Snowman had left the Lhotse Face almost ten years before. He had moved from the Himalayas when his food supply had run out. It had been a journey governed by primordial instinct, blindly, almost tropisticly. He had drifted down the East Siberian Sea, carried along by an iceberg which was moved by the current through the Beaufort Sea to North America.

Through Alaska, Canada, down into Washington and Oregon, he had gone in search of hunting grounds and the permanent glaciers which afforded him protection in the spring and summer. But he was always on the move, driven, searching for a more plentiful food supply and the frozen wastelands which his body required. For almost a year now, he had been embedded in a giant sérac in the California High Sierras. The supply of mountain deer and bears and the eagles which had their aeries below the summit had provided him with sustenance.

There had been virtually no snow even as the temperatures fell, and so he was secure. Snow threatened him, the strange menace of flakes zigzagging through the winds created a formation in the air which he could barely see. It aroused his fear, and on blind impulse he would leave the ice to strike wildly at the whiteness, the movement engulfing him.

Snow was his enemy, his constant antagonist. He

sensed that it waited, an ill-defined pursuer which had the power to destroy him. He had to fight that glistening white blanket which filled the sky.

Through the glaze of six feet of ice, the Snowman clawed his way to the surface, confronting his nemesis.

Janice's suite was on the first floor. Amid bouquets of flowers, bowls of fruit still covered in yellow cellophane wrap, she languidly posed in front of the mirror. The boutique inventory of size ten warm-ups, jackets, parkas, jumpsuits, and sweaters lay like a rummage sale on the king-size bed. In an improved temper, Janice pirouetted for Cathy around the room. Her breasts bulged out of a bra too small for her, and she made no effort to cover up when Barry poked his head in.

"Cathy, do they make thermal bras?" she asked.

"Not this year."

After the introductions were made and the principals identified, Cathy stood back and observed the prospective seducer and his victim smiling coyly at each other. Now if she could just get him to put those curves on skis and make a respectable pass down the beginners' slope, Monte would climb off her back and confine his attention to the sales team.

"Ever been on skis?" Barry asked.

"On water, around Catalina," Janice said proudly.

"Not on snow?"

"The only time I really truly enjoy snow is when I see it in the movies."

"Janice, why don't you get dressed and Barry'll take you out to the ski school and show you some of the fundamentals," Cathy said, carefully avoiding the word "teach" with its ghastly implications of working.

27

"You won't let me fall, will you?" Janice asked in a childlike voice.

His eyes moved from her face to the bed, then back again. "I'll be holding you," he said.

'See you two beautiful people outside in ten minutes," Cathy said. "We'll shoot some publicity stills of you and Barry."

"Thank God for sexual attraction," Cathy told Jim Ashby, who studied a press handout with Janice's biographical data and gave her a melancholy look.

"She was a cocktail waitress."

"A singing one," Cathy persisted. "Couldn't you stress the entertainer aspect of her career?"

"A singing waitress in a Santa Monica German beer garden? That's entertaining?"

On the ski-school slopes Barry and his pupil, who was on the short, one-meter skis, were staggering hand in hand before the lodge photographer.

"She must be a pretty fair piece of tail for Barry to make such a horse's ass out of himself," Ashby observed.

"That's what I sold him on," Cathy replied.

On the slope above them, Barry was trying to console and encourage Janice.

"Press your ankles forward till they rest on your boots. Weight on the balls of your feet. Don't move your upper body . . . everything comes from the legs."

She tried to digest the information as she clung nervously to his arm.

"You're going too fast and I'm afraid."

Barry skied midway down the mini-hill and extended his arms, but Janice remained rooted to the spot. She turned her head and watched small children skiing

28

down the icy runs. Their expressions of exhilaration and freedom apparently affected her. She turned her skis to the parallel position and skied down to Barry. In another moment the two of them were moving down together, and there was something touching about Janice's innocent elation.

"That's good—good—good," the photographer barked as he clicked.

"Before and after," Ashby said. "It's got human interest. You get yourself a Snow Queen and in ten minutes she's skiing. I'll do a spread with pictures and run a tear-out so you can use it for promotion."

The pieces were falling together, miraculously, Cathy thought, relaxing for the first time that day. Barry and Honeypie would look gorgeous in the color brochure, and sales would be bound to pick up.

"She's doing fine," Monte said, joining them. Accompanying him was Ken Atkins, his sales manager, a hangdog man in his indeterminate fifties who spent his days sopping up abuse from Monte because of the slow sales.

The company had expected instant success, for the rather naive reason that they had made a huge investment and wanted immediate returns on their money. But the sales matched the sluggish economy. People weren't quick to snap up Chamonix (the one-bedroom-and-loft apartment) or Innsbruck (two bedrooms and den) or the luxurious St. Moritz (three beds, den, and loft which could sleep twelve).

A fortune in advertising had been spent celebrating the virtues of Sierra, the quality of its buildings, the authenic Finnish saunas, the exciting night life at the Snowplow. What had induced people to come up for Thanksgiving was that fifteen chairlifts and gondolas were in operation, and lift tickets and ski instruction were free, while charter flights round trip from L.A., subsidized by the company, cost a mere twenty dollars. If they didn't pack them in for Thanksgiving, it would be a long cold winter. Cathy had persuaded Monte to hold a drawing and give a Chamonix model to the lucky winner.

But the weather refused to cooperate with them. Sierra had the highest annual snowfall in California, but this year the snows had been late and the lower slopes were barely covered for the opening.

Monte motioned her in the direction of the models, and Ken laggardly followed. A few couples were trooping in and out of the buildings with that detached, reserved air of lookers. Salesmen pursued them relentlessly with floor plans, literature, and offers of free hot rum toddies.

"Well, at least we've got Janice airborne," Cathy said, looking at the slopes and silently praying for snow. The clouds at the summit of the mountain were darkening, and the weather forecaster had promised a low-pressure system from Canada. But he'd been making the same promise for weeks.

"We still need some kind of media hype," Monte said.

"Opening a new ski resort isn't exactly network news."

In an effort to keep the pressure on her and saddle her with the failure of his salesmen, Ken broke the silence.

"Robert Redford. He's what we need, and he's a skier."

"He's got his own resort, and it's called Sundance."

"Competition's everywhere," Ken muttered darkly.

"Maybe you picked a bum sales team," Monte said, hitting his favorite refrain.

"Monte, they sold the ass off the Bahamas," Ken replied. "These guys moved land that was under water three hundred days a year. They ran inspection tours from boats!"

"Then why can't they sell our condos? The board let me drop the mortgages to eight and a half percent with five percent down. It's the best deal in the country."

"No one's disagreeing," Ken said.

"Do I have to bump up the commissions, is that it?"

"No, the men are hungry enough."

Chartered buses were disgorging hundreds of people behind them at the lodge. Soft flakes of lazy snow began to fall, and Cathy looked up with pleasure.

"God's on our side, gentlemen."

Near the summit of Sierra a violent cleavage occurred. The Snowman crouched low as the spears of iced snow pounded off his barbed trunk. His powerful hands crashed against a sangar, and loose stones were jarred and fell down the slopes. His rage was all-consuming, and he smashed everything in his path as his horned feet dug into the glacier. He began to climb down to the lower slopes, striding rapidly—in flight from the nameless enemy which implacably followed him. He paused at the edge of a snow bridge, then shielded himself in the hollow of a cornice.

In the distance were vague amorphous forms, and his roar was so deep that the snow bridge collapsed.

"Your progress is incredible," Barry told Janice. "Fact is, you're the best pupil I've ever taught." She was making fine looping turns. She'd be worth complete fidelity for the weekend, he thought, picturing her foot bath and a lengthy main event in the sack.

"It's like flying," she said excitedly. She had made two successful runs down the beginners' slope without a fall. "I love it."

/ Even the ride up the chairlift excited her. There were bright prisms of sunlight shimmering and forming rainbows above the peaks; a halo crowned the summit.

She turned to look at the lodge receding in the background. The chairlift passed over a large wooded area of serried Jeffrey pine trees. The branches rustled in the wind. All around them skiers in brightly colored outfits were going down the slopes. The snow was getting heavier, and she lowered her goggles.

"We can use this," Barry said. "It'll be packed by morning. Perfect conditions."

"Am I ready for the intermediate slope?"

"Let's see how you go on this run."

He leaned over the bar and pressed his face against hers. Then something caught his attention, and he pulled away abruptly.

"What's the matter?"

Coming into her view above them was a single ski. It gathered speed and flashed menacingly as it whipped past other skiers. She sensed the danger without understanding it.

"It's a suicide ski. Somebody's in big trouble."

The chairlift was nearing the get-off point for the intermediate slopes. Barry's body tensed as he searched the slopes for a struggling figure.

"Janice, stay on the lift all the way up. It'll take you down again. Just keep your poles on the outside," he said quickly, then glided off in a quick lithe movement to the booth placed at the get-off point. He signaled a man in the booth and shouted, "Call the ski patrol! I'm going out to look—"

She lost his words in the wind and craned her neck around to watch him sidestep up the slope past the booth. She adjusted the straps of her poles and faced front. The snow flurries were heavier as the lift moved higher. Sharp needles of ice were crashing into her face and bombarding her. The wind had picked up and scoured the flanks of the mountain with the loose falling snow.

It was becoming difficult for her to see, and she squinted through the goggles. The chairlift, caught in a wind current, began to rock wildly, and she grew frightened. As she moved higher, she saw that these slopes were deserted. The sky had turned an ominous slate gray. The mountain was darkening, and the increasing momentum of the snowfall had obliterated the runs. She waved at a solitary skier in the distance and called out to him, but the shrilling whine of the wind drowned out her voice.

"Get me off!" she shouted as the chairlift passed the booth on the advanced slope. She thought she made out a figure huddled in the booth. Above her heavy eaves of snow near the summit had been formed into cornices by the prevailing wind. The lift girdled the great façade of the glacier. The stark, glaring whiteness of the ice sheet blinded her, and her unease caused her to suck in great breaths of air, which burned her lungs. The rarefied air and lack of oxygen slowed her mind down.

It was unreasonable, this panic, she tried to tell herself. Soon she would be coming down and she would be safe. She was alone and she didn't want to think about it, but she couldn't help herself. Tears froze on her eyelids, forming hard crystals, and her cheeks were becoming numb with frostbite.

Higher up the storm had developed into a blizzard, the sheets of snow masking the relentless cliff lines. The ground below her seemed shaky. There were eerie, rumbling underground noises of ice movement, as if the mountain would cleave open and collapse in an avalanche. When the sky cleared for an instant, she saw a long sloping shelf leading to a vertical crack; the crack widened as she moved.

Her fingers were paralyzed from the cold, and when she attempted to bend them she realized that they were frozen. She almost blacked out in the thin air, but some deep instinct for survival enabled her to fight against the loss of consciousness. A sudden razor shard of light illuminated the summit of the mountain; she had the sense of relief which light inspires. For a moment she was entranced by the astonishing cascades of ice which stretched out in an unbroken line.

A series of triangular tracks resembling geometric rungs of a ladder created a rainbow mirage. As her eyes followed the clear line of the rainbow, she relaxed. She chided herself for her city girl's silly fears about what was nothing more than an extended amusement-park ride. Ridiculous.

In the distance beside the rainbow she thought she discerned the movement of light reflecting a shadow. She could see the complete Sierra range. There were hollow spaces beneath the cliffs, and narrow, twisting ice channels.

The shadow blended in with the ice; there was no contrast. It appeared to be traveling at the same speed as the chairlift, but then it loomed ahead, pulverizing the ice and creating fissures.

Something, she thought, was following her.

An unidentifiable sound echoed from below. For an instant it seemed to come from an animal: the deep enraged growl of a bear. It mystified her.

The chairlift dipped on its route to bypass a steep ridge that jutted up like a bent needle. The rainbow tracks were ahead of her on the other side of the ridge. Suddenly a beam of searing light burned her face; her goggles began to melt. She was too astonished even to cry out. The light vanished, and she wiped her face, blinking rapidly to enable her eyes to focus.

She saw reaching toward her a grotesquely shaped clawed hand. She swerved away, crashing into the metal pole dividing the lift. The fingers groped, and the form pursued her, keeping pace with the lift. She huddled against the bar. The fingers were upon her, touching her, squeezing the bone in her arm; she felt it splinter. A low agonized whine was the only sound she was capable of.

Her ski poles flew through the air; whirling along with them in free fall was her arm, ripped from its shoulder socket. A long plume of snow vapor turned a blackish red. Her eyes were closed. The hand clasped her right leg, and again disbelief was as intense as the pain.

Granitelike fingers held on to her torso. She forced her eyes open. Words were formed by her lips, but they were stillborn as the Snowman's grotesque massive face came closer. A series of gray-black veins snaked through the flat cheekbones, which were covered by razor-sharp pointed burrs. The nose was deeply recessed and virtually boneless, the forehead a series of angled rock-hard protuberances. The head itself was the size of a barrel and was set on the body with no neck. The gaping mouth opened and clasped her leg.

The snapping jaws echoed, opening and closing like some violent machine . . .

Janice was no longer anybody's headache.

Chapter Three

The snowfall built relentlessly, establishing a barrier around the lodge while the parking lot was still filling up with late arrivals. The turnout had been larger than expected. From a small wooden hut Cathy's assistants handed out mimeographed maps of the furnished condominium section which was set aside as rentals.

It was almost five thirty. The lodge lobby was crowded with those who had unpacked and were now exploring the amenities.

Cathy had been looking for Janice for the past hour: She was to be presented to the guests at a seven o'clock "meet and greet, mix and mingle" complimentary cocktail party given by the management. A Snow White evening gown still had to be fitted, and seven kids had been recruited to play the dwarfs.

Cathy searched the Snowplow Bar, now eight deep with merrymakers. She buzzed Janice's room again, without luck. Sierra's single dressmaker was becoming temperamental; she couldn't have the dress ready if Janice didn't report immediately for the fitting. As a last resort, Cathy tried Barry's quarters. There was no answer.

She went out on the terrace. A group of kids were sleighriding down the ski-school slope and throwing snowballs. Her name was paged over the P.A. system, and she went to the phone.

"Janice?"

"No, it's Monte. Where the hell is that idiot? She's due at the slide presentation."

"I've been trying to find her."

"Is she with Barry?"

"His phone doesn't answer."

"If he's honking her now, I'll have his ass on a skewer and he can pack it in and ski the hell cross-country back to Vail."

"Monte, I'll meet you at his place."

She hung up, zipped up her parka, and put on her hood.

The instructors were housed on the brow of a hill in the development's first building catastrophe, an octagonal affair shaped like a meatball and christened La Rosa Towers. It was unsalable and fit only for employee housing. She waited for Monte in the lobby.

His jeep pulled up, and he stormed down the corridor to Barry's apartment; Cathy had to run to keep up with him. A towel was knotted around the doorknob, indicating that Barry was inside and busy. Monte rang the doorbell. At the fourth ring, Barry came to the door, opened it an inch, and asked who it was.

Monte pushed past him, and Cathy followed reluctantly. Barry had a towel draped around his waist.

"Where's Sugarplum?" Monte demanded.

"Depends on who you mean."

"Janice," Cathy said.

"I haven't seen her since I left her on the slope. I took it for granted she was with you, Cathy."

"Bullshit," Monte said.

"Honestly, Monte. I had to leave her on the lift because some guy lost a ski; he broke his leg on Helter Skelter."

"You'll forgive me if I don't believe you," Monte insisted, thrusting Barry aside and throwing open the bedroom door.

Lying on the floor, her feet coiled in rope stirrups, her wrists locked in plastic grips, Linda Crown was doing a body-scissors exercise. Linda gave the under-six nursery-group ski instruction. Now she was naked, puzzled, but friendly.

"Where the hell is Janice?"

"Not here," Linda said, unthreading her limbs from the exercise rope.

Monte eased the door closed. "You were telling the truth."

"What's so astonishing about that?"

Monte turned to Cathy for assistance.

"I guess it just seemed logical that she'd be with you. We haven't been able to find her," Cathy explained, "and you had a bet with Erich . . . and I thought . . ." Cathy faltered.

"I had other things to do."

"But how could you just leave her?" Cathy asked accusingly.

"Don't tell me my business. Someone out on the run with one ski takes precedence. Anyhow, Janice was doing fine—and she was on the chairlift. Now why don't the two of you shove off."

* * *

A sense of foreboding governed Cathy's actions. She spent the next few hours going through the lodge with several instructors, searching for Janice. They checked the bar, and had Janice paged at fifteen-minute intervals. The local taxi-service dispatcher sent messages to his drivers, giving Janice's description; the car-rental agencies and the airport were also questioned. In desperation, Cathy decided to visit the condominiums to see if Janice had by some chance run into a friend and was having an innocent drink. All the while Cathy greeted new check-ins, was battered by tiresome questions about linen, firewood, and mealtimes. Dozens of times she passed the lines outside the main warming hut, where people waited to get their boots and be fitted with skis. Occasionally a smart-ass would shout out to her—"Did you find *him* yet?"—which heightened her tension and became a jangled refrain.

By ten that night her nerves were gone. A desolate, unremitting voice within her insisted that Janice was out there, buried under the lashing gale of snow which had begun to fall that afternoon. Heavy gusts of wind thrashed the loose drifts.

In a daze she accompanied Monte to the airport. The snow came down in blinding, torrential sheets. The chains on the tires of the jeep made a ratcheting sound, carving through the high drifts which had accumulated on the road since that afternoon. She lighted a cigarette for Monte and passed it to him. Sudden wind gusts forced the jeep into dangerous slews. Cathy was strapped in by the seat belt, but she held on to the roll bar.

The temperature had dropped sharply to fifteen below zero, and the heater droned, fighting a losing battle with the condensation that fogged the windshield. Cathy wiped it with a sodden chamois cloth.

"Christ, it's horrible to think of her on the mountain. But where else could she be?" Cathy said.

They parked in front of the air traffic control building and made a dash from the jeep. The building shuddered from the impact of the wind through the open door. Monte's pilot was huddled in a corner of the room, sipping black coffee out of a plastic cup. He had a disgruntled look on his face.

"Is there a chance that the airport'll open up?" Monte asked.

Stan, the traffic controller, a pudgy middle-aged man who looked as though he was merely in attendance until the fishing season began, yawned and said:

"What kind of a fuckhead are you, Monte? Didn't you hear that the Japs disbanded the kamikazes? You hate Chuck or something? We'll be lucky to open the airport by tomorrow morning. There's a sixty-mile-an-hour wind from the southeast and visibility is zero. If you could take off, where would you land, in Acapulco?"

"I wanted Chuck to take the chopper up."

"Mr. Dale," Chuck protested, "we'd be blown apart. There's an ice storm at five thousand feet with slabs the size of barn walls."

"Ice sheets, Monte. Just as a matter of curiosity, where were you planning on going at twelve o'clock in a copter?"

"To the advanced slope."

"Cathy, who's been spiking his drinks?" Stan asked.

"The advanced slope of Sierra!" Chuck repeated, as though to confirm that he was in the employ of a sadistic lunatic.

41

"Monte, what is it with you? You been pissing and moaning that you haven't got enough snow and that the resort's going to die stillborn. Now that you've got more snow than the whole state of Colorado, you become suicidal," Stan said.

"Why up there?" Chuck asked.

"There might be a girl up there," Cathy said.

"Did you do a bed check?" Stan asked skeptically.

Chuck nodded. "Mr. Dale, even if we could get a copter up there, how'd we cover the mountain? The lights we've got aren't high-intensity. It'd be like using a flashlight."

"Monte, there's been eighteen inches of snow down here since this afternoon. Multiply that by five and you got seven and a half feet of snow at the summit. If she's up there, it doesn't matter now. She'll be buried."

The ugly reality of that possibility gnawed Cathy all night long. She sat in her living room with a bottle of brandy at her feet, staring into the log fire. She hadn't liked Janice, and the guilt she felt was oppressive. She and Janice were two opposing forces, but once there had been little difference between them. This partially explained Cathy's well-concealed animosity. Elements of the girl she had been six years ago, when she was nineteen, were reflected in Janice, and Cathy despised the vision of herself that Janice represented.

Cathy had messed around when she was younger in a series of painful affairs. Now she had little respect for men, since most of them were in search of an easy piece, mothering, or both simultaneously. Her job demanded the front of glibness, friendliness, and she fell into the role rather than expose her vulnerability. She had mastered the shades of public relations, which she understood as civilization's method of counterfeiting reality.

When at last she dragged herself to bed, she resorted to the lapsed Catholic's final appeal. She dutifully kneeled on the floor and prayed for Janice. Hypocrisy had the slender virtue of shielding a troubled conscience.

Chapter Four

The morning had a biting frost along with a clear sunny sky. Plaques of ice hung outside Cathy's bedroom window, then dropped onto the sill. She was startled from her sleep by the voices of men outside. She got out of bed, shuddering from the drafts that came through the sloppily caulked walls.

A party of ski instructors led by Barry and Erich were carrying their equipment to the gondola shed. Monte was maneuvering a snowmobile up the slope, which had hardened overnight and now shone like glass. The rainbows flashing off the belly of the slope were hauntingly beautiful.

Cathy dressed quickly, swallowed a cup of instant coffee, and pulled her skis out of the rack by the front door.

When she reached the gondola, Pat Garson, the town sheriff, looked quizzically at her. His connection with crime was limited to examining hunting and fishing licenses and giving offenders citations; he wrote out the occasional traffic ticket and rescued lost hunters. He somehow managed to keep in the public eye.

"You going up, Cathy?"

"I thought I would."

"Think she was lost in the storm?"

"It looks that way, doesn't it?"

He put an OUT OF ORDER sign outside the gondola and joined her inside. The car moved slowly on the cable. The wind had subsided. At the ten-thousand-foot level towering Lodgepole Pines by the side of the runs made a frieze; they seemed placed there for decoration. The rock needle above the advanced slopes with its overlay of ice and its darker sedimentary border was stark white and suggested a massive ivory horn jutting out from the mountain.

They got off at the upper slopes. Monte had set up a communications post outside the control booth at the gondola get-off point. Static cracked over the radio as he listened to Chuck reporting from the helicopter. Above them the chopper was being buffeted in the winds.

"This is Northern One. Anything, Chuck?"

"Not a thing."

"Can you drop your ceiling?"

"I'm catching crosswinds. Any lower and I'll lose stability."

"Over and out," Monte said.

Cathy spotted Ashby talking to the instructors. Wherever Garson went, reporter-publisher Ashby was sure to be around. He had endorsed the sheriff's last four election campaigns, writing editorials for him and functioning as his campaign manager. He felt there was nothing tangibly dishonest about his spirited partisan attitude, since it encompassed the boundary of friendship. Besides, he knew the townspeople seldom believed what they read about the sheriff. So Ashby would make Garson sound like Wyatt Earp when he discovered a stolen car, Sherlock Holmes if he uncovered stolen property, and on the few occasions when prostitutes wandered into the town from neighboring lumber camps he would proclaim, SHERIFF GARSON CRACKS VICE RING, thus enabling Sierra to doze peacefully under its blanket of morality and purity.

Garson opened a large metal box and handed out flare guns to the instructors grouped around Barry. Barry pointed down the icy run.

"I left her just before the intermediate slopes. She could have taken Mambo, Stump Alley, or even Rickshaw down to the lodge. Now fan out and try to keep at the same speed when you go down. If there's any sign of her, fire your flares."

The instructors began the downhill run, spread out in a wing formation.

"What do you think happened?" Ashby asked Cathy.

"I don't even want to guess."

"With all the new snow, it might be summer before we find her," Garson said.

"If she's up here," Monte interjected optimistically.

Ashby picked up Monte's binoculars admiringly: an expensive pair of Zeiss, 50 x 50 power with a 200mm zoom lens. He scanned the mountainside, then held on the summit.

"Crazy," he muttered. "Must be light refraction." He handed the glasses to Cathy. "Look up to the summit."

Cathy adjusted the focus. She was startled by the series of large rainbow-colored triangular shapes which appeared to be embedded in the ice. She searched above the cliff line for a triangle which could be forming the design. Monte took the glasses from her and followed her direction, then went to the radio and instructed Chuck to drop down over the northwest base of the summit. They watched the copter circle and disappear from view over the blind side. A moment later Chuck's voice came over the radio.

"Golden shit bricks . . . tracks, dozens of them. I'm going in for a closer look."

"Can you photograph them?" Monte asked.

"I'll try."

They waited for more details but were unprepared for the panic-stricken report.

"The tracks are smoking—they're on fire. My instruments are going bananas. Caught in turbulence. Leaving the—" His voice trailed off, breaking contact.

The helicopter came back into view, listing wildly in the crosscurrent. It hovered overhead now, its rotors churning.

"Chuck, what happened?" Monte asked over the radio.

"I don't know. My instruments went crazy and my compass stopped working. There was some kind of magnetic interference. I'm going to do a sweep over the lower slopes."

"Did you get any pictures of the tracks?"

"I sure hope so, because I'm not going back up there."

The instructors were skiing slowly, wedelning in large rhythmic turns just below the expert slope. They were growing tired, and Barry signaled to them to descend lower. He stopped at the edge of the tree-lined cross-country trail. The incline provided a better perspective on the mountain below.

Out of the corner of his eye he saw a broken ski pole at the foot of a red fir. He skied over to it. There was a churning in his stomach. Beside the pole was a glove, stained a maroon-black. It had frozen. He nervously scanned the underbrush but made no move to investigate further. He felt warm and uncomfortable as his pulse rate increased. He peered up the tree in a posture reminiscent of a shy girl.

On a branch he saw something, yellow.

Bile gathered in his throat, and he moaned an indistinct "Shit." His muscles rebelled, refusing to obey him, and he struggled with the flare gun, eventually firing it. Then he sat down on a tree stump and closed his eyes.

There was a frightened silence when the men gathered in the area Barry had signalled from. They looked up at the tree, unable to comprehend the bizarre sight that confronted them. A few of them grunted and coughed nervously.

Garson unloaded a long aluminum pole from the top of the snowmobile that had been sent down to bring up the coroner. He brought the pole to the tree and shook the branches. Lodged in a nest of branches some fifteen feet above them was the yellow object, which he was able to shake loose. It thudded to the ground, and the group of men turned away. The parka sleeve was spattered with frozen flakes of blood.

It was an arm.

Cathy forced herself to look.

The coroner circled the tree, then stepped out of the men's view. For a moment he couldn't bring himself to speak.

"Pat, Pat, over here." He directed the sheriff to a

high clump of branches. The two men stood staring above them at the grotesque vision.

Garson struck the branches again with the pole. The tree seemed reluctant to give up its secrets. Cathy watched from behind them and felt a wild panic which transcended fear. Somehow, she was in the country of the unknown. She wanted to scream. As her eyes roved the deserted slopes, the intense loneliness of the frozen mountain enveloped her.

What they were all observing hardly seemed possible. But the horror was there, and they were held, mesmerized, by the sight.

Janice's head dropped from the tree and bounced on a shoal of ice.

The coroner stood some distance from it as though contact would infect him. Janice's face was barely recognizable. Her right eye had been torn out, livid black six-pointed stars seemed to have been branded into each cheek. The top of her skull was a dark cavern of mutilated tissue. The head had been ripped from the girl's body. Shreds of darkened nerve endings protruded from the neck cavity.

Barry moved away and leaned against a tree. His body rocked involuntarily, and tears formed in the corners of his eyes. If only he'd waited for her to get off the lift.

When the coroner could speak, he told Garson and the instructors to dig for further remains.

Cathy followed Monte and Ashby into a clearing. Ahead of them triangular tracks led through the woods, then disappeared.

Up close the tracks were enormous, almost four feet long from the base to the apex. Within the base there were innumerable deep indentations.

"Could this have been some kind of bear?" Monte asked.

Ashby looked doubtful. "When a bear walks, it steps down on the entire sole of its foot like a man. It's called plantigrade . . ."

"But we've got silvertips and grizzlies up here," Cathy said.

"What kind of a bear burns black stars into human flesh or makes tracks like this?"

"What if the tracks aren't connected to this?" Monte asked. "Couldn't this be some kind of chemical reaction from the soil erosion or the blizzard?" Ashby shook his head. "Let's assume," Monte persisted, "Janice is sitting on the outside of the lift. A sudden wind swirl hits her. She stands up or tries to get off, and she falls at great speed into the branches, which decapitate her and rip her arm off. Maybe there is a bear in the area and then he attacks her . . ."

"Anything's possible. I've seen lots of dead people when I've covered stories . . . but this is just beyond me."

Unless he had the support of other specialists and/or elaborate laboratory tests, the coroner was reluctant to offer even the simplest ideas with which to explain a cause of death. Dr. Sam Powell, after endless consultations at the Sierra General Hospital, which specialized in the instant repair of skiers' broken arms and legs and overflowed with orthopedic surgeons, finally revealed the results of the post mortem he had performed on Janice Pace.

With the interested parties assembled at his hospital office, he was still afraid to commit himself in front of Ashby, the sheriff, and Monte. Monte was in attendance to gather a firsthand account for the board of directors, who would demand an explanation.

Dr. Powell began with a cautious disclaimer.

"This is still unofficial, gentlemen, but we've got a medical oddity here."

"Shit, Sam, a gunshot wound's a medical oddity to you," Ashby complained.

Powell lit a cigar and then poured his guests large shots of Harwood's Canadian Whiskey. He sipped his drink reflectively, adjusted his glasses, and opened up a folder with Janice Pace's name on it.

"I've had a neurologist look at the remains of the skull and the chief of orthopedics examined the limb . . . which is all that we found. There's no way we can determine the cause of death. My first thought was that she somehow got caught in the chairlift machinery. But there are no traces of severing by a machine or a blade of any kind."

Powell carried his drink to a blackboard behind his desk and drew a head and an arm with its socket.

"If it was a bear, where are the teeth and claw marks? And then there are those star burns on the skin. No animal I know can inflict those, and it wasn't done with acid." He pointed to the blackboard. "All I can say for sure is that the poor girl had her arm *ripped* off at the articular cartilage here. As for the head, it was yanked off at the thyroid by something with incredible strength. This exposed the cervical nerves and the ganglia. The nerve centers were in shreds. Beats me how her head was taken off." He passed the bottle around, and the men refilled their glasses. He opened his desk drawer and took out a piece of string, then snapped it in half. "That's what happened."

Ashby had filled three pages of his notebook, and he stared at the new blank page.

"Sam," he asked, "do you have any theory, no matter how wild, about how she died?"

"Not a one. The head and arm were found almost thirty feet above ground on the tree branch. How did they get up there?"

"What's the death certificate going to say?" Garson asked.

"Misadventure."

The *Sierra Messenger* office was in a small wooden building on Canyon Drive, Sierra's main street. The paper had originally been a camping journal, listing backpacking routes, beauty spots and views for the amateur photographer, and desirable locations for hunting and fishing. In 1945, when Jim Ashby returned from four years in the Marine Corps, he had enrolled in a correspondence course in journalism given by the University of Missouri, and then taken over the paper. He was determined to provide the town he was born in and loved with a real newspaper, offering town and national news of interest to the locals.

He ran the paper with two printers and an elderly secretary who had been a librarian in L.A. before settling in Sierra. He was the paper's astrologer, art and book critic, cooking authority, financial analyst, and political gadfly.

Unfortunately, the most popular column in the paper was one that he treated with contempt and had begun as a practical joke. It was called "Strange and Unusual Occurrences from the Unknown" and written by Ashby under the name "Mandrake." The material that appeared was invariably filched from the country's major newspapers.

At dinner that evening with Pat Garson at the Horse-shoe, the two bachelors stared at their bowls of chili. The very act of eating seemed disgusting. They were both overcome by the horror of what they had witnessed. Ashby's mind had wandered over the events of the day. Several times he lost the thread of their conversation, and he sat distracted by the fire, staring at his brandy. His mind was attempting to focus on some elusive memory that tantalized him, and when he finally finished his drink, he knew he couldn't play the usual game of three-cushioned billiards with Pat. Specters of the girl's severed head floated through his consciousness.

He returned to his office, filled the potbellied Franklin stove with coal, and sat at his large roll-top desk with its covey of pigeonholes. It offended his sense of factual reporting to begin digging into the storage cabinet that contained the columns from the "Unknown." At his insistence, his secretary had never wasted her time organizing this material.

Ashby carried out stacks of dogeared yellowing files and patiently thumbed through them. At eleven that night he had reached the mid-1960s. His slipped disk was acting up, and he was forced to read standing at the printing press to relieve the pain. But he was convinced that somewhere buried in the pile was a mention of those strangely shaped tracks. Under a sheaf of papers, his eyes blurring and squinting, he found the columns for October 1966. Along with his original article, he located the sources for it. The first was from the Associated Press. It was headed:

DANIEL BRADFORD RETURNS
FROM EVEREST WITH
TALL SNOWMAN TALE

Daniel Bradford, the young anthropologist and Rhodes Scholar, recently returned from an expedition to Mount Everest. The expedition was funded by private sources from the Los Angeles Explorers Club. According to the club members the purpose of the expedition was a search for the Abominable Snowman or *Yeti* as it is known among Sherpas.

Bradford, 26, who was the Olympic Bronze Medalist in the downhill ski event at the 1964 Olympics, made a series of unsubstantiated claims.

He said: "We were attacked at the Lhotse Face by a Snowman. It was impossible to gauge the size of the creature because of the way he blended in with the ice. My guess is that he was twenty to twenty-five feet tall. We had followed his tracks from Nuptse across the Western Cwm of Everest. The tracks were enormous, perfectly symmetrical triangles which threw off a multi-colored light and there were horned marks within the tracks.

"The attack," Bradford continued, "took place during a blizzard at Lhotse. The snowman literally tore apart the members of the party and the Sherpa porters. He ripped their heads off, hacked their bodies and then began killing animals in a frenzy.

"His jaws were larger than a whale's and his mouth was filled with innumerable rows of sword-shaped teeth that were almost a foot long."

Apart from Bradford, the only living member of the party was his guide, Pemba, a Sherpa porter who unfortunately spoke little English. Both of them were rescued, Bradford said, by a cult of Buddhist lamas who lived in a cave and worshiped the Snowman, Bradford revealed a large black star-shaped scar on his right shoulder where he says he was clawed by the Snowman.

Bradford's account was met with skepticism by the members of the Explorers Club, and there were motions to censure him. One member, who wished to remain anonymous, said, "He ought to be expelled for insulting the membership with this outrageous justification of his panic and coward-ice. Nineteen people died. He was the leader of the party and he ran out on them, and don't let anyone tell you different."

Chapter Five

After a sleepless night, Jim Ashby reexamined the files
he had uncovered on Bradford. He sat down at his old
Underwood typewriter and inserted a piece of paper;
then he moved away from the table. There were of
course similarities between the attack Bradford had
alleged had occurred and the remains he had seen of
Janice. But they did not constitute hard evidence. If the
news were leaked, journalists from all over the country
would descend on Sierra and the media with their teams
of researchers would swallow Ashby's story. He had a
proprietary interest in keeping his suspicions and the
facts secret.

Under the guise of sleepy small-town newspaperman,
Ashby concealed an intense ambition to excel, make a
national name for himself. An exclusive story—one
which he could control—would be worth thousands
of dollars. He saw his byline in the London *Times*, *Le
Figaro*, the *New York Times*; he would be a guest on all
the major talk shows. Carson and Merv would listen
raptly with mouths open as he related the story. He

could become a celebrity. Fate had singled him out as the reporter to investigate what might turn out to be the single most important news event of his life. He had to find Daniel Bradford.

He wouldn't botch it. He returned to his typewriter and wrote two lines about Janice Pace being lost on the mountain and the coroner's verdict of misadventure. It would run in Saturday's edition. It would arouse too much attention if it were on the front page or beside the local TV listings, so he buried Janice in a squib below the obit section. His readers would pass quickly to Mandrake or the chilied-lamb-shank recipe.

He gathered his articles and the photographs of Janice which Pat had allowed him to study. He packed a suitcase, then put on his single city suit, a shiny blue serge, and his Marine rep tie. He'd change from boots to shoes when he got to L.A. He called his office and told his secretary that he'd gone for a few days, but he would check in with her every evening.

He pulled the choke out on his Cherokee, listened to the engine's bronchial rumble, and set off on his mission with the stealth of an assassin. He drove past Pat's office and was tempted to stop for a moment. But his journalist's instinct of always listening to a confidence but never giving one made him push down hard on the accelerator.

The Explorers Club occupied a massive Tudor-style house on Rossmore in Los Angeles's serene Hancock Park area, and Ashby parked in the lot beside the house. A caretaker raking leaves squinted at him and said, "Safari?"

"No, I'm a climber. Himalayas." That as a back-packer in the summer he had never gone higher than four thousand feet along wide trails hardly mattered.

"I'll show you to Mr. Ravel's office."

According to one of the articles Ashby had seen, George Ravel had been responsible for Bradford's expulsion from the club. Ashby would have to be careful questioning him. He was led into a wide circular corridor. A display case held a variety of vipers, and he looked with interest at his first deadly krait snake. The heads of lions, tigers, panthers, and leopards were mounted on the walls. Beside Ravel's office there was a giant stuffed gorilla with a deep barrel chest. It all struck Ashby as quaint, remnants of a bygone era. People took cameras on safari nowadays, not rifles.

Ravel was one of those rosy-cheeked, heavy-set men with the bluff manner and capacity for earbending that Ashby had encountered among local fishermen. He'd spoken about the club for a good five minutes before Ashby was able to interject a word.

"I'm planning to climb Nuptse this summer and I need a damn good guide."

"Well, I can fix you up with some Sherpas in Katmandu."

"Any of your members interested?"

"No, they just like to shoot. I'll check our files. There is of course a fee if we put the party together for you."

"I assumed as much."

As Ravel went through a file of index cards, Ashby noticed that the caretaker was eavesdropping, dusting a display case at great length.

"I've heard about an American who's supposed to be good," Ashby said.

"Which one?"

"Daniel Bradford."

Ravel's manner changed abruptly. His anger was choleric, but he subdued it.

"You must be joking. That bastard lost his entire party in 'sixty-six. You might as well climb with a murderer."

"What makes you say that?"

"Listen, when nineteen people die on a climb and one comes back with a story that a ten-year-old wouldn't swallow, any normal man would be suspicious."

"I've read about Bradford. What's your theory?"

"I think he went crazy and murdered a few of the people with him, then he led the others to a point where they couldn't climb along Lhotse and he deserted them."

Ashby continued to prod the delicate nerve.

"But wasn't he the best climber we've ever produced?"

"That may have been, but the man was insane." He glanced at a card. "I can recommend Geoffrey Griggs. He was picked by Edmund Hillary for the World Book Expedition but broke his arm before they set off."

"When can I meet him?"

"When you arrive in Katmandu. Griggs lives there now. I can send him a cable and he can arrange everything for you—porters, equipment."

"I'd hate to fly all that way and find that we weren't compatible. At least if I had Bradford's address I could interview him and make up my own mind."

"You're just looking for trouble, Mr. Ashby. If you want Bradford, then I won't be the one to tell you where you can find him. I don't want you on my conscience."

"I'll think about Griggs."

As he walked back to his Cherokee, Ashby was aware that the caretaker was behind him. Ashby turned and suddenly felt uncomfortable. The old man seemed overtaken by an inexpressible fury. His hand quivered as he pointed toward the club.

"Don't believe that lying son of a bitch," he said. "He'd never accuse Bradford to his face."

"Then why—"

"They had an argument. Ravel was against Dan from the beginning." He took out a piece of paper and scribbled down a barely legible address and handed it to Ashby.

"What's he doing on an Indian reservation?"

"I don't know. I've forwarded his mail there for years. If you see him, tell him Andrew sends his regards."

"Was he really as good as the papers claimed?"

"Sherpas said he was the greatest climber who ever lived—better than Hillary."

Ashby's interest was deeply engaged. The conflicting accounts of Bradford he'd heard suggested that he was tracking a strange and extraordinary man. Why, he wondered, did a man of such accomplishments drop out of sight and settle among a tribe of Indians, banishing himself to a life of obscurity?

At Monte's insistence, Cathy had flown down to Los Angeles with him to discuss Janice's death with the board of Great Northern Development, the resort's parent company. The company headquarters were in Century City, on the twenty-sixth floor of one of those faceless towers which had sprung up in the last few years. The boardroom, a multiwindow affair with a hundred-and-eighty-degree view of the city, dazzled her, but when she saw the indignant expressions on the five men sitting at a long Italianate glass table, she ignored the view. The men did not bother to stand, and Charles Wright, the chairman, waved her to a seat between two secretaries. He simply nodded at Monte, who joined the others at the table.

"Monte said we've got some kind of public relations problem up at Sierra," Wright began. He had shark-gray eyes, a crab-shaped body, and one of those slick tennis tans that end at the neck.

"I checked with the paper; Ashby put in a two-line obit about the girl," Cathy informed him.

"That's excellent." Wright looked pleased, but she seemed unresponsive. He asked, "What's bothering you?"

"Ashby left town . . . I don't think he's going to quit on this story. I think he wants us to believe he's going to let it go. It's a smokescreen."

Wright shook his head in dismay. "Well, for Christ's sake, fix him."

"How do I do that?" Her voice was losing its timbre, disintegrating. Wright frightened her, and the silence of the other directors was equally unnerving.

"We've got a fund for that reason."

One of the other directors suggested that they buy out Ashby's advertising space for the next six months.

"Ashby's one of those small-town editors," Cathy explained. "Integrity's his stock in trade. I'll have to finesse it, put it on a personal footing."

"Anyone else trouble?"

"The sheriff," Monte replied.

"He's Ashby's closest friend," Cathy said.

"Will he keep his mouth shut?" Wright asked.

"Only if Ashby tells him to," she said.

Wright opened a black folder and looked at an information sheet listing the town officials.

"Garson's just a rubber stamp who Ashby backs each election." His gaze fell on Monte, and he pointed accusingly at him. "Didn't I tell you to buy that fucking rag before we broke ground in Sierra?"

"Charlie," Monte pleaded, "he wouldn't deal. The alternative was to start a rival paper, and none of us knows the first thing about running a paper."

Wright's tan was fading, and he ran a hand through his tinted hair.

"The two of you listen. I want that son of a bitch Ashby sandbagged. I don't care what you have to do." He paused and reached for a cigarette, which he placed in a Water Pik filter; then, after lighting the cigarette, he removed the filter and threw it against the window. His secretary got up from the table, picked it up, and handed it to him.

"Do you want a Valium, Mr. Wright?"

"No, my wife got tickets to *A Chorus Line* and I want to stay awake for the first act." For a few moments he stared blankly at Cathy. No one uttered a word. "Cathy, if some kind of panic breaks out in Sierra, we'll lose twenty-five million dollars. Christ, I never should have allowed us to get into this."

"Charlie, it'll be okay. I'll handle it," Monte said, hoping to reassure him.

Wright glared at the other board members.

"We'll never cross-collateralize again. God, to think that we borrowed money from our own savings-and-loan to finance this project, and then, to compound things, our own insurance company has to make the payout! What'll it run?" he demanded.

"About two hundred thousand," Bill Hammond replied. He had devised the scheme of providing mortgages through the savings-and-loan for approved buyers at the resort. The mortgage business was more profitable than the actual sale of the property. "A quarter of a million if the girl's parents kick up a fuss."

"Maybe the legal department can beat them down on the settlement," Wright noted.

"Let's not look for trouble with them," Monte said.

As Wright rose to leave, Monte caught his eye, indicating that there was more to come. It was for Monte a delicate and dangerous moment. His career might collapse on the basis of the material he had prepared. The photographs of Janice's remains and the tracks would be construed as shock tactics. These men could be easily unsettled when faced with the grotesque realities, and he might compromise his position with them. Fear dictates its own laws, and Monte was in a terrifying bind. He opened his attache case and took the pictures out.

"Christ, this is gruesome," Wright said, and hurriedly passed the photographs on, then gesticulated futilely to Monte. "You said on the phone that some kind of bear was loose. Did a bear kill her?"

"I don't know. The tracks weren't made by any animal we can identify."

Wright poured himself a glass of water from a silver thermos and popped a Valium into his mouth.

"What's up there?" Hammond asked nervously. "I was going to send my kids to the lodge for Christmas."

"Cathy, we'll make whatever money you need available. You don't have to account for any of it. It's all in cash—but somehow you've got to find a way to contain this."

Wright rose from the table and moved sluggishly toward the door.

"I've never seen anything like this," he muttered.

Chapter Six

Holiday Inns were all the same; no surprises, ran the commercial. Ashby checked into the one in Westwood. His room looked as if it were made out of disposable plexiglass. They probably just threw the whole thing down the incinerator when the guest left.

Ashby had spent the afternoon at the AAA trying to figure out a route to the reservation. It was inaccessible by plane. Forty miles from Blythe, it showed up as a minute crescent in the heart of the Mojave Desert. The Colorado River angled through it, but there was no sign of a road.

He phoned his secretary and learned that the only newsworthy event was the merciless snowstorm, the heaviest one of the winter thus far. The balmy late-Indian-summer weather in L.A. was a relief.

"You've had calls from Monte and Cathy all day." He was not surprised. "They've been on my back about your story on the girl."

He poured a Scotch from the pint of Dewar's he had

bought before checking in. No point in paying room-service prices.

"They give any reason for being so concerned?"

"Not to me."

He swallowed some Scotch. It was wise to play possum.

"Margaret, call them back and read them the obit. That should calm them down. Anything else happening at the lodge?"

"Not that I've heard. It's packed. Seems all the advertising they did paid off."

Over a cold hamburger in the coffee shop, the vision of this mass of visitors rushed through Ashby's mind, and his unease increased. Weren't they all in danger? But if he warned them off, he might be starting needless hysteria. He had no proof of a Snowman—would have none unless Bradford could identify the marks on the body. Besides, he wasn't sure he believed it himself. Wasn't the only Snowman ever seen thousands of miles away in the Himalayas? Did the creature have the ability to reproduce?

In the moonlight the ski lodge was the size of a small pearl from the glacier below the summit of Sierra Mountain. A thin, veinlike crevasse slowly appeared in the glacier. It gradually widened as the fissure expanded, heaving blocks of ice as large as ten-story buildings down the mountainside. New ice channels were forming between the pinnacles of snow, and troughs belched forth as boulders were shifted and trees uprooted. The rumbling sounds could not be heard eighteen thousand feet below at the lodge, and in a few moments the tremors became muted in the vicious hacking of the wind.

Under the surface, frozen rock was being crushed. An opaque light, gray and diffuse, began to sear the frozen ice cascades. An arm sprang through the melting glacier, and the Snowman emerged.

He moved downhill toward the lodge. He took huge strides, and the ice hissed from the heat given off by his body. The blizzard conditions near the summit drove him into a frenzy. He had come down thousands of feet and was now just above the advanced slope. In the distance the lights from below formed a darting jellied viscous pattern. His attention was diverted by the whipping of the cables which the gondolas ran on.

The wind changed direction, and now on the mountain there were other sounds which were familiar. In the guttural rasp of the eddying winds the roars of bears were carried as they prowled the dense forests. He took the scent and hacked down a large fir tree. Intruders threatened his hunting ground.

Ashby started out at six the following morning, to avoid the downtown freeway traffic. The distance to the Desert Center was about two hundred miles, but he had no idea how long after that it would take to reach the reservation. He stopped off at a roadside deli and bought himself a couple of sub sandwiches and a six-pack of Coors. He rolled down all the windows, because the heat was becoming intense. When he reached the desert, sand devils struck his car unexpectedly, causing it to veer from side to side. In the distance, smoking, swirling tornadolike winds rose from the flats as though from a witch's caldron, whipping the sagebrush and yucca. There was a constant hum over the baked terra-cotta arroyos and then the sudden swoop of a shrike and its vicious "chack" as it attacked a spadefoot toad too slow to reach its burrow. Waterless stream beds twisted down the slate mountains. Along the roadside behind cacti tortured into peculiar shapes were rattlers, lizards and Gila monsters. The windshield was smeared with a variety of fire ants and centipedes blown from the ground by the sand devils.

In all the years he had been a reporter, his curiosity had never been so powerfully aroused by a man. It was beyond him to understand how a man like Bradford had given up civilization for this barren life. Bradford's retreat struck him as not only unreasonable but also enigmatic. He could not reconcile the idea that a Rhodes Scholar and an Olympic skier could end up in this desolate no man's land. He was determined to find out why Bradford had punished himself this way. Was he in fact a murderer and this a form of penance?

The glare of the sun became relentless, and after a while the shimmering effect dazed him. He had left the main road and was bouncing along a primitive dirt track. Nothing, he thought, could survive in this heat. Some miles farther he was forced to change his mind. On the roadside was a battered whitewashed adobe hut. Several Indians with washed-out hooded eyes and hardened leather skin toned to dark copper regarded him with a hint of curiosity. Indian jewelry, pottery, and blankets were displayed beside the hut in a fruitless commerce.

Ahead of him, like a group of lost, haunted souls, were a number of Indians working with primitive axes and shovels on a road. Beyond them the road was well made, with a tarred surface. Ashby drove past them along the verge.

The Indians, stripped to the waist, wore ragged shorts and tattered shorn jeans. Sweat gleamed from their chests and backs. They seemed indifferent to his arrival.

The sun had set moments before he reached the entrance of the reservation. The ride had been a nightmarish experience. He had crept along at five miles an hour over the steep rocky trail, which was deeply rutted and a nesting ground for snakes, lizards, and hordes of flying insects which flew at the car in throbbing, maniacal formations as though unleashed like a biblical plague. The Cherokee was caked with mud and patched with dead insects.

Ashby was directed to the Indian agent's house, a log cabin leaning over a high bluff. The agent was a lean, squinting man by the name of Dennis Crawford. He was obviously so pleased to learn that a civilization of sorts still existed that he smiled idiotically at Ashby.

The amenities he offered were minimal: a drafty curtainless bathroom; a group showerhouse, where the water smelled strongly of sulfur; a dinner of greasy salt pork and beans; and enormous shots of raw whiskey in chipped mugs. Crawford also arranged for a group of Indian children to wash Ashby's car.

Whenever Bradford's name was mentioned he fell into a moody reflective silence and drank more whiskey. It wasn't clear if he was playing a poker hand and trying to get paid for information or if Bradford held some power over him.

"When do I get to see Mr. Bradford?" Ashby asked.

"He's not back yet."

"How do you know?"

"The Indians never begin prayers without him," Crawford said obscurely. Then he lapsed into that faraway, dazed posture which shelters old drunks unaccustomed to company. "You'll see something damned peculiar soon as he comes . . ."

At the end of the day the group of men working on the road took their reward in the stream just below the reservation. They peeled off the pickup truck like new recruits from boot camp. They picked up cans of beer from a case which had been left cooling under a large rock at the mouth of the icy stream. Their bodies were smeared with dust, muddied from sweat, and they plunged into the water. They babbled and sang like boys, scrubbed each other's backs with thick borax soap until their skin tingled. It was a fine time, the best part of the day for them. They discussed their progress, which was measured in feet. To build a road without heavy equipment was an accomplishment each man took pride in.

They would spend perhaps half an hour in the water and behave as though they had not seen one another for months. It was impossible to talk in the sun. The effort was too great. Grunts, nods, the occasional question was the extent of their conversation. In the evening, the apparently stolid nature of the men gave way to free joyful expression. When they left the water they would lie on the straw-hard burnt scrub to dry off and drink some more beer. The road would not be mentioned; it was bad form.

The men drove up to the reservation, refreshed and happy. In the last light the fields of vegetables and fruit were an eyesore, hard arid ground which provided bare sustenance to the people. Their diet relied heavily on beans and rice, and some of the children grew up with rickets. In a small compound a dismal attempt was made to raise chickens, but the scraggly birds squawking in the pebbled, muddy runs were undernourished, good only for boiling. Yet another fiasco, the men recognized, were the thirty head of cattle they had purchased from a bankrupt rancher. Agents from the Department of Agriculture had promised to send them feed, but none had arrived, and the cattle, subsisting on burnt grass and shrubs, bellowed hungrily in their stalls.

On the field that ran along the cabins, small boys were playing football. Bits of rag and chamois pads had been sewn together by the women to outfit them with uniforms. A misshapen bloated object was flung through the air and bounced crazily on the ground, and both teams scrambled for it. The women watched for the men over their crude charcoal braziers. Beside them on wooden poles trout hung drying. Everywhere the eye traveled the landscape of poverty incarcerated the people.

Yet when the men arrived the spell of deprivation was broken. An odd aura of joy infused them. The sound of a drum, monotonously and primevally rhythmic, was heard. The children cleaning Ashby's car began to run in the direction of the drum and Ashby shouted after them:

"Hey, I thought we made a deal—a buck a head . . ."

The car was clean in sections, but crazy-quilt smears still disfigured it.

"Save your breath," Crawford said, "they're going to their prayer meeting. They're crazy—mad, I tell you. I can't control any of them."

"Who?"

"Bradford and the Yaqui. They converted the whole bunch of them to some kind of religion. Mystical . . . I don't understand any of it."

"Who's the Yaqui?" he asked as Crawford rubbed his rheumy eyes and dispensed with the task of civility by pulling from the bottle.

"He's what they call a sorcerer. Bradford's his disciple," he added ominously.

Below them, in a large circle around a tent made of lizard skin, were the Indians. Two men joined hands and moved to the center; they both held torches. Then, at some signal, the entire group broke into an eerie chant.

"Om Mane Padme Om . . ."

They repeated the words endlessly until the sound became a low hypnotic wail.

"It's like this a lot of the time, but then sometimes they all go for days without saying a word," Crawford said. "Silence . . . total silence. Scares me."

"Why do they do it?"

"I don't know. I've been on other reservations, and this one's different. It changed when Bradford and the Yaqui drifted up from Mexico some years back. They brought some kind of mushroom with them, and they chew it. Gets 'em high for days. They get hallucinations and run around naked, screaming." He paused and stared at him helplessly. "Bradford once told me that they're entering God by eating the mushroom—a sacred mushroom God. They're insane. If you knew what was good for you, you'd get the hell out of here."

"Bradford was a mountain climber once," Ashby said. "He led a party up Mount Everest."

"Don't surprise me none. He goes on retreats with the Yaqui up Palomar Mountain." He indicated a stark black outline silhouetted by moonlight. "They don't carry no food or water, and they go barefoot," he added incredulously.

"According to what I heard," Ashby continued, "Bradford let his party die. He panicked and ran out on them."

The agent wheezed, and a spume of phlegm gathered in his throat. Ashby realized that he was being laughed at.

"Bradford's a lot of things to the people around here, but I never heard he was a coward. Last year a bunch of FBI agents come up here and arrested the Yaqui. They claimed he was dealing dope. Well, there was one hell of a fight. Six of the Utes were shot— massacred, if you want my opinion. But they didn't get away easy. They lost two of their agents. They arrested Bradford for it and kept him in jail for a few weeks, but they couldn't find any witnesses."

"Did Bradford kill the FBI men?"

"If I knew, I wouldn't say."

Chapter Seven

Bradford sat cross-legged, balancing a tin plate with charred trout on it. He hadn't touched his food. He waited for the Yaqui. The old man came out of his tent, frail and limping. His white beard, which had been full and shapely when Bradford had first met him in Tuxpan, ten years ago, now resembled the frayed ends of a knotted rug. The eyes were deep-set and in the firelight were like irregular anthracite pebbles. The Yaqui had not been eating, and Bradford was worried about him. It would be humiliating and disrespectful to attempt to feed him, and he would be rejected. The Yaqui was his guide, and their roles could never be reversed.

Their relationship could be traced to Bradford's return from Everest with the story of his encounter with the Yeti. The media and his colleagues had built a wall of ridicule around him, destroying his self-confidence, until Bradford reached the end of his own resources and began to doubt his own experience.

A gradual process of deterioration as insidious as an

unidentified virus had finally worn Bradford down. He had no choice but to disappear. He signed on as a hand on a tramp steamer and spent a year as a seaman sailing the Punta Mayo and Juruá rivers of South America, collecting rubber from plantations. From there he had wandered through the interior of Mexico, eventually arriving in Tuxpan, where he was arrested for vagrancy.

He and the Yaqui met in prison, and spent months together in the same cell. When he joined the Yaqui on a pilgrimage through the Yucatan Peninsula, Bradford had slowly regained a semblance of his self-respect. He embraced the Yaqui's mystical beliefs, and when they wished to commune with the sacred soma they chewed the divine mushroom of immortality.

But even during those periods when he was hallucinating—freed from reality—the primitive urge for revenge still haunted him. The ineradicable specter of the Snowman was still buried in his subconscious. Thrusting through the ice were the distended spikelike fingers, the teeth which ground so that hard sparks flew from them, the horned skin and the massive head. He had seen nature's ultimate savage kill his men. The cataclysmic violence of the Snowman during those last few hours would never leave him.

Bradford had left his environment, forsaken friends and colleagues, and entered what he recognized as a fugue state. He suffered occasionally from a loss of memory because the pain of the past was too intense to tolerate. But in spite of the Yaqui's guidance, Bradford knew that he could never enter the state of perfect tranquility until he could vindicate himself. One day he would return to Lhotse.

An Indian boy brought a plate of filleted, mashed trout for the Yaqui, who said: " I'm fasting, you eat it."

The boy took the plate away, and Bradford watched him hurry back to his brothers and divide the portion among them.

"I'll join you," Bradford said to the Yaqui.

"You spent the day working and you're hungry. You'll always be a disciple and never a master," the Yaqui said.

"Why?" Bradford asked without emotion.

"You imitate too perfectly and try too hard for unity. Trying is resistance to the idea of embracing God. Only when you yield will you succeed."

The Yaqui invariably spoke in riddles; when Bradford had been a young college student he had been skeptical of precisely this aspect of religion, the naive and simplistic explanations that passed for profundity. Bradford had not been able to restrain his logical mind, and although the Yaqui had virtually resurrected him spiritually, he still held back the total commitment to the mystical deity.

The Yaqui stared at him, then shook his arm when he did not respond.

"Daniel, I had a vision last night," the Yaqui said in a low, troubled voice. "You were on the snow and blocks of ice were falling. Men were dying . . ."

In the flickering campfire Bradford imagined that he saw the faces of his dead Sherpas. The impression was so strong that he jumped to his feet and stumbled backward as though retreating from some invisible force.

A small Ute boy studied him and peered around him to see what had caused his reaction. He looked up at Bradford and saw nothing, only the mantle of darkness.

"Mr. Bradford, the agent said there was a man up at the post who wanted to speak to you."

"Is he a Fed?"

"I don't think so," the boy said, scampering off.

Bradford walked along the rutted path snaking through the compound. Men finished with their dinner sat smoking around the dying fires. Their resigned faces altered and they greeted Bradford as he passed. He was popular with them, but their affection toward him was inhibited by a certain fearful respect. Bradford did not approve of fighting for trivial reasons. The previous week he had caught two men quarreling over a pack of cigarettes. He had fought both men, using his knowledge of karate and judo to throw them and hold them up as examples to the others. Some of the Utes resented Bradford's skill and the humiliating spectacle of a man no bigger than either of the two Indians thrashing both of them until they pleaded with him to stop.

He climbed up the steps of Crawford's porch and made his way into the cabin.

"Are you Daniel Bradford?" Ashby asked.

"Yeah."

Ashby extended his hand and introduced himself.

Bradford moved to the range and poured himself a cup of coffee, then walked around the room like an animal in search of a resting place. He perched on the edge of Crawford's camp bed.

"There's some chili beans, Dan, if you're hungry," Crawford said.

"I've eaten."

"Well, I'll leave you two and make my rounds."

Bradford was tall and muscular, and his face was a mahogany hue from the years of sun. His blue eyes were washed out, and they had a certain evasiveness that Ashby had encountered in fugitive drifters. He had a broad nose, and his skin was drawn tight as a drum. He wore his dark brown hair shoulder length, and it was highlighted by blond sunstreaks. He looked like a half-breed.

He stared at Ashby, unnerving him.

"What are you, a narc?"

"No, a newspaper editor. I've had a hell of a time finding you."

"Maybe you shouldn't have bothered. If you want to know what happened to those two FBI men, you could've saved yourself a trip. I've got nothing to say. In any case, you guys never write the truth."

Ashby smiled; he had Bradford at a disadvantage. He settled down at the table and poured himself a drink.

"I don't give a damn about the FBI," Ashby informed him.

Bradford seemed skeptical. "Really?"

"That's right. I don't know what the circumstances were that caused your trouble, but I wouldn't believe either side. If you killed them, that's your business."

Ashby detected surprise behind Bradford's stolid expression. He always studied a man's eyes, never his face.

"Fair enough," Bradford replied.

"The fact is, the two people I've spoken to about you warned me I was going to meet some kind of psychopath."

"Well, Crawford's a pisspot of booze. He's scared shitless of his own shadow, and he'll say anything."

Ashby drank slowly, letting Bradford wait. It was good to be away from Sierra as a working reporter using his wits to squeeze a story out of a man.

"George Ravel was sober when I spoke to him."

He dropped the name casually, but he was fully aware of the impact it would make. The key to Bradford was to keep him off balance. Bradford came toward him, lifted him off the chair, and shoved him against the wall.

"I'm not here to fight you," Ashby said.

"Then what the hell do you want?"

"I want to use you," he admitted.

Bradford let go of him and circled the room. Ashby observed the mood swing. Bradford now appeared subdued and confused.

"Ravel?" He shook his head uncomprehendingly. "Why? I hope you're not trying to dig up bodies from the past."

"Andrew said to send his regards. He still believes in you."

"Mr. Ashby," Bradford said in a low, quivering voice, "don't look to cut my belly open."

"I've got a problem—"

"Don't we all."

"You're the only living expert—"

"I've been through this before," Bradford protested.

"Look, let's work together. We both need each other," Ashby began. "I haven't taken the trouble to locate you just to rake up a ten-year-old story. I've brought some photographs I want you to look at . . . but first I'd like to know one thing. Would it be possible for the Snowman to have left the Himalayas?"

Bradford stared vacantly through him.

"Sogpa . . . Sogpa . . . Sogpa."

"What are you saying?"

"The lamas called him Satan."

"Mr. Bradford, a girl was killed in Sierra. She was on a ski lift. When we discovered her remains, no one

knew what to make of them. The coroner took the safe
way out and ruled the death misadventure. Frankly, I
wasn't satisfied. So I went through my files. I'd run an
old story on you from the wire service in which you
described the Snowman. Well, the similarities between
your account and what I saw on the mountain were so
close that I had to track you down."

He handed Bradford the photos of Janice's head with
the black stars burned into her face. The other photographs were close-ups in color of the triangular footprints.

"Christ," Bradford said, "he's on your mountain."

He pulled up his denim shirt and turned his back.
Standing out like a raised birthmark was the same star
Ashby had seen on Janice.

"I had three skin grafts and that's the best the doc-
tor could do. When the skin heals, it re-forms into this
shape."

"You're sure you saw the Snowman?"

"My Sherpa did as well." Bradford placed the pictures face down on the table. "What do you want to
do?"

"Trail him," Ashby said.

"You'd need a team to go up after him, and equipment. But you're not in shape. You wouldn't last five
minutes on the mountain."

"What would you suggest?"

"You're after a story—I want to hunt him down and
kill him."

"How?" Ashby asked.

"I'll find a way."

The Snowman climbed along a sloping shelf in the
forest, and his feet petrified the snow and ice into gro-

tesque molds. A high screeching roar commingled with the wind striking tree branches and resonated when the wind subsided until it seemed as though a giant female Kodiak were being mimicked.

The roars were answered, and rushing up the façade of a precipice were two male Kodiaks, sexually excited as the love calls became more passionate and insistent. The claws of the Kodiaks dug into the ice, scraping a path along the cliff lines. The bears, frost coming from their mouths, were aroused and sniffed the air for the scent of the female. They stopped on a moraine, which was an accumulation of stones and debris brought down by the glacier.

The two bears now confronted each other. They were almost the same size and weight, one just about ten feet on its hind legs and weighing something over thirteen hundred pounds. Its competitor in the pursuit of the female was more than eleven feet and weighed almost fourteen hundred pounds. The largest known living flesh-eating animals on the face of the earth were without the knowledge of fear.

They roared menacingly at each other. The smaller one raised its front paws to attack. In that instant it was seized from the moraine by its head, and as it thrashed the air viciously the Snowman crushed its head in his mouth.

The other Kodiak immediately began a retreat. It scampered exhaustedly away from the massacre until it reached a couloir. It took refuge in this gulley in the mountainside. It had stopped to rest, bellowing breathlessly, when it was plucked from the deep furrow by its hind legs. The Snowman's claws probed the soft belly of the bear. Still alive, its intestines exposed, the Kodiak gave a low, groaning sigh, ululant and yielding, as the Snowman impaled it on his horned chest. His teeth dug deeply into the bear's head and ripped through the skull.

Bradford lived in a tent next to the Yaqui's. It was without comforts, and all he could offer Ashby was a place on the canvas floor. A smoking kerosene lantern with a blackened wick threw off flickering tongues of light.

Ashby observed a canvas camp bed, a sleeping bag, a pair of worn boots, an old backpack, some denim shorts, and a torn work shirt drying on a clothesline. The mean smell of poverty pervaded the tent.

"Any idea of what an expedition would cost?" Ashby asked.

"Thousands. No one'd make that kind of investment in me," Bradford said without self-pity. "Not again."

"Suppose I had access to money people."

"How'd you get them to part with it?"

Ashby wondered about the value of candor at this moment. Perhaps it might be best to be straight with Bradford, so that there would be no misunderstandings later. Bradford unquestionably could be dangerous. There would be no way to control him unless a bargain was struck at the outset.

"A major corporation owns the ski resort. They've spent something like twenty to thirty million—no one knows for sure—developing the resort and putting in runs and lifts. They've built town houses and condominiums. Some bad publicity and they'd have a hell of a lot of trouble finding buyers."

"You'd blackmail them."

"Well, that's a little severe, don't you think? I prefer to think that I'd be performing a public service by warning people about the dangers on the mountain. After all, a girl was killed by an unidentified creature."

Bradford smiled.

"Would they bite?"

"I'm going to try it on."

"And what do you expect out of it?"

"Fame and fortune—the usual things that small-town nobodies dream about. I'm a newspaperman. I've been reporting broken legs, car skids, the weight of babies, high-school football scores, and weather for most of my life. This story fell into my lap. I can't hack it with the networks or the major papers. If they start sending up journalists, I'll wind up running their shit. This story would make my name. If I have to squeeze somebody's balls, then I'll do it."

Bradford didn't take the bait. "Nothing could persuade me to take you up with me. One weak man and we'd all be dead."

"Okay. But what I'd expect would be an exclusive story. We'd set up a radio with the ground. I'd be at the other end with my tape recorder, or following you with a helicopter when I can, taking pictures. I'd want one of your people to carry a camera with him."

"You're crazy, you know that," Bradford stated.

"Not really—just hungry . . . like you." Ashby rose and stretched his arms. "There'd be money in it for you."

"I'm not interested in the money."

"Well, maybe the people here would be. You might get a score yourself and then give it away. I don't give a damn what you do. But it seems to me I saw you and those Indians out in the sun trying to build a road. You'll never finish it without a Cater and a steamroller. You'll be dead before you've got twenty miles laid."

He studied Bradford's reaction, and he knew that he had driven the man into a corner.

"When I was at college I read some Sinclair Lewis. He used to write about hypocritical small-town sons of bitches like you."

"Only difference, Mr. Bradford, between what you read and me is, I'm the real thing. Now, is there anything like a telephone in this wasteland?"

There was one in Crawford's cabin, and Bradford listened as Ashby went through a series of roles: irate public-spirited citizen ("Somebody's got to be the conscience of the community"); investigative reporter ("The public has a right to know what's up on that mountain"); extortionist ("Well, I'll just have to contact the networks and the wire services. I'll let them make their own judgments on the basis of the evidence. I'm with a man named Daniel Bradford who was attacked near Everest. He's identified the footprints and he's also got a scar on his back that's exactly like Janice's").

"Monte, if you want to be chintzy, that's your problem. But lookit, you're a public company, and I'm sure the SEC would want to investigate your property development after they see the papers. Now, I've put a call into the Forestry Service in Sacramento. I'm going to request that they send some investigators."

Ashby also demonstrated that he was a shrewd negotiator.

"No, I don't think two hundred and fifty thousand dollars is exorbitant. If GND found that they could buy a gold mine tomorrow in Eagle Mountain they'd be there with the cash. Now, you've got the number I'm at, so if I don't hear from you in ten minutes I'll start making my calls."

He and Bradford settled down on the porch with a bottle of Crawford's redeye. Ashby placed his old Bulova on the rail so that he could read the luminous hands easily.

"Will he go for it?" Bradford asked.

"I don't know. Big corporations are usually gutless. They can stand up to people their own size, but the little man frightens them."

Ashby swallowed the redeye without blinking. The emotional high and sheer intoxication of power overwhelmed him. If only he'd discovered this years before, he might have become really important, someone he himself could have respected.

"Dan, do you think the Snowman can be killed?"

"Yes."

"Twenty feet tall . . ." he began, then trailed off.

The phone rang, and Ashby signaled Bradford not to pick it up for a few moments. On the fifth ring, Bradford picked up the receiver.

"Yes, this is Daniel Bradford. Who's this? Okay, Mr. Wright. I'll meet them at Eagle Mountain. It's about five hours from Los Angeles. No, he won't make any calls tonight."

Ashby's laughter was roisterous and infectious.

"Scared him shitless," he said. "I should've asked for half a million."

Chapter Eight

Cathy and Monte took turns driving on the miserable trip through the California desert. They always kept sight of the armored Wells Fargo truck accompanying them. Guards had come to the GND office that morning, and Wright had handed over the money without a word. While the guards waited outside, checking their route, Wright had cautioned them both.

"This money doesn't exist, is that clear?" They nodded. "It's bad enough Ashby's got us on the run. But if he finds out about our emergency fund, we'll have more trouble than Lockheed ever had. I don't know if this is some kind of elaborate scam and if Bradford's his partner or if they're seriously considering going up the mountain. I hope for Ashby's sake he's not taking us for a ride, Monte. And I want you to make it very clear to him that if he's playing games, we'll get our money back."

It was early afternoon when the dusty, mud-spattered Seville and the Fargo truck pulled into the ghost-like main street. Eagle Mountain was a little rathole lodged in the middle of the desert. Although the town was on the Colorado River, it was nothing more than a mud bed.

They passed a clapboard general store with a wooden porch on which food lay exposed on metal trays. Squadrons of large desert horseflies flew sorties over the food, but the Mexican tending the scales and the Indian women on line stoically ignored the sunbaked brownish beef spoiling before their eyes. A bit farther along, at a two-pump gas station, a grease-stained Indian mechanic sweated over a primitive rusted pickup engine. Beside the station was a hardware store with a battered sign advertising Remington guns.

The truck slowed down and one of the guards peeked out of a slit at an adobe building with a grimy storefront window on which a shaky signprinter had scrawled "RESERVATION BANK." In front of the bank, Bradford stood waiting. A guitar case was at his feet.

"What the hell are they going to do with a quarter of a million in this garbage dump?" one of the guards asked.

"Maybe the Indians struck oil," the driver replied, parking in front of the bank."

The rear doors were opened and the guards with their M-15's resting in the crooks of their arms waited for the driver to bring out the steel cashbox. He walked between the guards toward the bank.

Bradford watched them and smiled slyly, disconcerting the guards.

"You got nothing better to do, mister?" he was asked.

"I'm just waiting around to make sure the count's right," he said.

Ashby stood by the bank door, gullies of sweat pouring from his cheeks and gathering on the limp collar of his shirt. "Where'd you go, by way of Mexico?" he growled at the Fargo guards.

"We ran out of freeway fifty miles back," the driver replied sourly.

The heat was oppressive and burned Cathy's nostrils when she stepped out of the air-conditioned car. The glare hurt her eyes, and she put on her sunglasses. Ashby gave her a friendly wave.

"Jim," she said angrily, "I never expected you to pull this kind of stunt. Why didn't you tell me what you were going to do?"

"Cathy, you're bright and pretty, but you're an employee. You didn't have the authority to come up with the money."

"Are you serious about going up the mountain?" Monte asked him.

"Not me. But Mr. Bradford and a team he'll recruit are going to find out how Janice was killed."

Cathy looked at Bradford. He had a serenity about him that was unnerving and, she thought, somewhat patronizing. He was nothing more than an itinerant cowboy, one of those white Indians she'd read about.

"I'm Daniel Bradford," he said affably.

"The bank manager can count the money, Dan," Ashby said. "Let's all get out of the sun and have a beer."

There was a small cantina at the end of the street. It was cool and dark inside. An old fan droned monotonously, and the radio was tuned to a Mexican station. The bartender brought them bottles of Dos Equis, which he kept on a block of ice; they dripped on the scratched wooden table when he set them down. Bradford was seated next to Cathy on a rickety backless bench, and she felt his leg touch hers. She and Monte listened to his account of his search for the Snowman; then Ashby pulled out the newspaper articles, which were impossible to read in the dark bar. What impressed her about Bradford was that combination of sincerity and fanaticism that she had encountered only at school in Marymount. The religious zeal of the nuns had oppressed her. Bradford's gods were dark, and he was ruled by an obsession. He was not really interested in the money and she regarded this as a sign of arrogance.

Ashby was more transparent. He wanted a story and he didn't care who he had to sacrifice for it. The ruthlessness of small-town provincials had an element of corruption about it that was more insidious than the big-city variety, since it had a single source. What troubled Cathy was that a pattern of conspiracy was emerging in which she would have the central role. Bradford might go up the mountain, but she would be the one to perpetuate the big lie. Others might die later or even now, and she would cover it all with a web of deception.

"If we accept this story about a Snowman—and you've got to admit it's a lot to accept," Monte began, "how can we be sure you'll succeed this time?"

"What's your option?" Ashby asked.

"They could call in the National Guard," Bradford said. "Just imagine a division of them in Sierra."

"The evidence is all circumstantial," Cathy interjected. "We've handed over a quarter of a million dollars in good faith, and Mr. Wright doesn't care whether you find a Snowman or not. The story's got to be buttoned up. Contained, Jim. And I don't know that I'd take your word on anything."

"You can have your money back," Ashby countered. "I'm not getting any part of it. I can't afford a leak either. If we're all being selfish, my best interests are served by keeping the media out of it. Which is why I just threw the story away in two lines. I don't need anyone asking questions about a mystery death."

"What about the sheriff?" Monte asked.

"He's in my pocket," Ashby replied. "Now, if you're satisfied that this isn't some rip-off, Bradford and I ought to get started."

Monte nodded to her. As they got up to leave, she could not refrain from asking:

"What made you ask for that precise amount of money?"

"Ashby asked for the money."

"What are you going to do with it?"

"Split it five ways. I figure that's a reasonable price for a man's life."

When they were outside, he opened his shirt and pulled down part of it, exposing the scar on his shoulder.

"Does it look familiar?" he asked Cathy.

The sight of it shook her, and she defensively put her hand up to her eyes. What she had seen on the mountain would live on within her.

"Why are you going?"

"I want to kill the Snowman," he said with profound conviction, as though this was his quest, his passion.

The savagery of his reaction was virtually sexual. She had never encountered a human being with such a finely tuned attitude of naked violence. It took her out of her own corporate sphere, where men were just as dangerous but were capable of modulating their desires, finessing their enemies by the astutely planned maneuver. Daniel Bradford stood exposed, baring his teeth and carrying a spear for the world to see.

"You coming in to count your money?" Monte asked, thrashing the air at mosquitoes. Bradford shook his head. "Well, are you going to deposit it?"

"No, why bother?"

"Do you mean to say that you're going to walk around with it in cash?"

"Sure, who's going to take it from me?" he asked without concern.

"What if you get held up?" Monte asked, looking perplexedly at Cathy.

"I'll take the chance."

Bradford was handed a clipboard by the Wells Fargo guard, and he signed his name next to the entry "Received cash $250,000 denominations $100." After agreeing to meet Cathy and Monte back at the reservation after he had gathered his team, he took hold of the metal box and threw it in the back seat of the Cherokee. He picked up his guitar case and unceremoniously slid it alongside the box. Then, as they all waited for his next move, Bradford yanked the tab of a can of beer and climbed into the back seat.

"We've got a long ride, through the desert up to the Arizona border," he told Ashby, who was going with him. "It's just past Yuma. A place called Bard."

He sipped his beer slowly, relaxing like a seigneur accustomed to the attentions of an entourage. Bradford noticed Cathy looking with curiosity at his guitar case, and she finally asked, "What sort of guitar do you play?"

"I don't play," he replied. He lifted the clamps of the black case and pulled up the lid. She felt her saliva dry up, and she forced herself to smile pleasantly at the two sawed-off forty-gauge shotguns fastened to metal racks in the case. They were as awesome as pythons.

Chapter Nine

The seven mustangs in the corral were listless and hungry. Bone protruded through their withers, and their ribs pressed tightly against the flaccid skin of their sides. Ed Packard had served in Vietnam for three years as a weapons expert in Special Forces, but during the whole nightmarish experience he had never conceived of the horror that he now faced.

He would have to kill the mustangs.

He had nursed them as yearlings when he bought the ranch two years ago with the savings he had accumulated after his discharge. His dream had been to leave behind the bitter memories of a wife who deserted him and the rat race of Los Angeles, where he had worked as a Physical Education teacher in an elementary school.

City people are sustained by fantasy, and Packard was no different from most. Locked in freeway traffic each day, he felt his need for privacy, a retreat away from the crowds and cars, become more urgent. One day he had picked up and roamed through the western states until he found the piece of land that divine providence had selected for him.

It was a foreclosure, and the bank offered him reasonable terms. He put down fifteen thousand in cash, took out a second mortgage, and saw himself as a gentleman horse rancher who would hunt and fish throughout the year. Idylls such as his, unless backed up by substantial financial reserves, tend to go sour. The inexperienced city man fell prey to larcenous horse traders and unscrupulous feed merchants, not to mention the drought which burned out his rich grazing pasture. Packard's credit soon ran its slender course, and he was shunned by the local tradesmen and harassed by the bank.

Yes, he would kill the horses rather than see them sold for fifty dollars a head when he knew they'd be worth a thousand apiece if they could be properly fed. He'd been up all night brooding, and when he walked out of the barn carrying his loaded Rossi Overland .20-gauge hammer shotgun, he was tempted to turn the weapon on himself. The horses straggled to the fence posts and whinnied pathetically when they saw him. Dumb stupid beasts who depended on him; he loved them all with a strange, inexplicable ardor.

He heard a truck engine behind him, and he wheeled around with the shotgun stock pressed into his shoulder and knew that he'd fire if it was the bailiff, a fat, tobacco-chewing soak, who'd served him with writs twice before. He'd pour kerosene on the body and he'd just hang in and wait for the locals to prove he'd done it.

He sighted the Cherokee and released the safety, then suddenly lowered the weapon as the truck splayed pebbles from the driveway. The people in the wagon had to be lost. In his desperation he considered robbing them and stealing the wagon, which he could sell to settle his debts. But he pointed the gun at the ground and masked his panic with a welcoming smile.

When the door opened and he saw the tall man with the burnt skin emerge in his faded Levi's and denim shirt, he was startled by this unannounced reunion with the man who had trained him to mountain-climb before he'd been sent to Vietnam.

It had been at an Indian reservation where Bradford and a Sherpa had been civilian instructors for the Special Forces unit which had been assigned to the Golden Triangle in Laos. Packard had dropped Bradford a few letters when he had bought the ranch, inviting him to stay there for as long as he liked. But Bradford had never replied, and Packard had simply ignored the slight. Now he approached Bradford with his hand extended.

"What'd you do, strike oil on the reservation?"

"Not yet, but we're still praying," Bradford said, looking at Packard's drawn features and the embittered, forlorn cast of his mouth. He seemed whipped and scared to Bradford. "How's the horse business?" he asked out of courtesy, when all around him the acrid smell of failure hung like stale air before a thunderstorm.

"I've got my ass in a sling and it's getting kicked so often I don't feel it any more."

"How much are you stuck?"

"If you're lending, well, twenty-five hundred would get my head bobbing over the waves."

Bradford looked at the baked red clay hillside, the starved horses, the ramshackle cabin, and knew that Packard had been burned out.

"Can you get your horses boarded somewhere?"

"Why?"

"I want you to go on a skiing vacation with me—all expenses paid and fifty thousand dollars for your end."

"You wouldn't shit an old friend, would you, Dan?"

When Bradford pulled out a fresh stack of hundreds with a band around them indicating that the bundle contained five-thousand dollars and then handed the money to him, Packard shook his head uncomprehendingly. The gift made him edgy and uncertain, and he rubbed his dry, cracked lips with a trembling hand.

"Who do I have to kill?"

"I'll let you know when I'm ready," Bradford replied.

It took several hours before Packard could make arrangements to have his horses boarded at a large neighboring ranch. He tethered his horses and rode with them in a file down the road to an open corral, where two hands took them. The bank manager was surprised by the cash payment he made to settle his arrears, but he made no effort to question Packard. He deposited the money to Packard's account and wrote down his instructions to pay the bills Packard had accumulated in town. He hoped he'd never see Packard again. These surly Vietnam veterans were a different, violent breed.

The three men made East Las Vegas in three hours flat. The Cherokee wagon cruising at ninety was as comfortable as a club chair. Bradford had tracked Spider Howard to his last known address: the county jail.

Spider had served with Packard as a demolitions expert, then had taken a job as a security man at Caesar's Palace. But the temptation to find a method to beat the tables had been too powerful for him to withstand. So Spider had developed the infallible "Spider Craps Percentage System." And after a spurt of small wins he had eventually crapped out, to no one's surprise but his own.

With the connivance of the call girls who visited the conventioneers' rooms at the hotel, Spider had burst in on passionate dentists, rueful Legionnaires, and pleading Shriners and insisted that he had to report them to the management and of course the vice squad. Fifty, a hundred, or whatever he could wheedle from the distressed but willing-to-pay victim had provided Spider with the stake necessary to resume rolling with his modified system. But then an East Las Vegas detective who'd heard a series of complaints had checked into the hotel, playing the John role with the muddled helplessness of Jack Lemmon, and when Spider entered to rip his eyes out, Spider's days on the badger circuit had ended.

It was $1,500 for bail, a $500 fine or sixty days. Spider was now in his thirty-sixth day in the county jail, and he often thought with fondness of his time in Nam, which in his imagination took on the patina of glory days during which he had acted with conspicuous bravery, blowing the V.C. apart with his armory of high explosives. He had sent a pleading telegram to Packard, who responded with an apologetic postcard that the walls were closing in on him.

When the car pulled up to the jail, Ashby began to wonder not only about Bradford's sanity but about his own.

"Do we really need a criminal?" he asked.

"Come on, Jim, relax. Spider was just pulling a scam

and got caught. It wasn't anything like some of the rip-offs you must've seen in your time."

Bradford paid Spider's fine, which was reduced because of the time he'd served. The bony black man now had swabs of gray in his thick hair. The smile creases were tight pockets lodged in his face like cheap tailoring. Spider was surprised to see Bradford, and he kept up a steady gabble of questions as he checked the envelopes with his personal effects. His cash, a five and four singles, looked thin, mean, and faded when he tucked it into his wallet.

"Why'd you put up the money?" he asked as they walked toward the gate.

"You still remember how to climb, don't you?"

Spider pointed to the walls of the jail. "I couldn't handle these."

"Well, we're going climbing, and you'll be paid fifty thousand for your part."

"Man, I been layed, relayed, and parlayed in Vegas, so don't play games with me."

When Packard showed him the roll of cash, Spider knew that his luck was about to change.

The guard who escorted inmates in the exercise yard watched the money display, then shook his fingers across his belly as though cooling them.

"You mean to say we had Lou Brock here and never knew. What next, Spider?"

"Ann-Margret on a toasted bagel," Spider said.

"Can't kill fuckers like us," Packard said.

"You the rich uncle?" Spider asked, peering at Ashby.

Bradford's lone dissent prevailed against the three others: No, they didn't have the time to spend a night on the town in Vegas. They would have to head west to China Lake just above Fremont Park for another man in the crew Bradford was building. Packard took over from Ashby, who had been caught nodding at the wheel. Packard, like a boy experimenting with his first set of wheels, kept the accelerator down at an even one twenty.

They reached the isolated cabin by the side of the lake. A small wooden sign with childlike block letters crookedly printed on it stated:

EXPERT GUIDE
Fishing and Hunting

Across the lake in the last bands of afternoon sunlight two men with hunting rifles and a third who was unarmed stood motionless as though captured in a stone frieze. Bradford and Packard left the others to walk off their stiffness and cut through the underbrush toward the hunters. The rustling of dried leaves and fallen branches distracted the hunters, who turned to the source of the sound.

"Game warden?" one of them asked the short, lithe, slender yellow-skinned man who wore a tightly bound long black pigtail.

"The game warden is away. His brother takes his place, and he runs a store in town. Never comes around." He peered at the ground. "The tracks are hard. They'll be coming down for water soon."

Along a ridge beyond the lake a small herd of Sierra mule deer stood circumspectly, sniffing suspiciously at the air. A lead buck clambered gracefully ahead. The hunters were paunchy, middle-aged, wealthy men with English Purdie .30-.30 rifles, bedizened in suede jackets

101

and leather cartridge bandoliers. They struck Bradford as absurd, perpetrating fraud in their role as sportsmen. Two of the cows were pregnant, and the bucks' antlers were re-forming after the seasonal shedding.

Bradford and Packard stepped into the clearing, and the hunters, momentarily distracted, turned when their guide put his fingers to his lips. They fired wildly, missing the cows which had wandered down to the edge of the lake.

"You ruined our shot!" one of the men barked furiously.

"You couldn't hit a duck's ass if it was sitting on your plate," Bradford said.

"Give us the guns," Packard said.

They took the guns from them, and now the deer were running flat out in high, loping, rhythmical movements, as though attached to springs.

"I'll take the lead stag," Bradford said. "You get the buck at the end."

Two shots rang out, piercing the tranquil stillness of the woods, and two bucks fell silently on the other side of the lake. He and Packard dropped the guns in the soft mud of the bank. A school of minnows formed a black mass as they swam away from the noise. In the middle of the lake hungry bass leaped out of the water. The hunters started off through the muddy shallows for the fallen bucks.

"You just cost me a day's pay," Pemba said with irritation.

"Since when did you become a hunting guide?" Bradford asked.

"When I stopped eating *tsampa* and found I preferred steak. What are you doing here?" he went on, overcoming his indignation. "I've been pleading with you for years to come here and work with me. We could have built a real business." Pemba had remained in the States, and still had visions of becoming a capitalist and returning to Namche Bazar, the village he was born in, with a fortune.

Pemba stared at Packard, trying to place him; then, unsettled, he turned to Bradford for some explanation. There had to be a good reason for Bradford to leave the reservation. When his shoulder was touched by the familiar hand of his friend, images of their past together and the tragedy they had witnessed on Lhotse burst to the surface. Pemba had spoken little English when he arrived with Bradford in the United States, and he had been battered by questions which he could not understand when he attempted to corroborate Bradford's account of the disaster.

Now Packard shook his hand and said:

"You and Dan trained our unit on the reservation, remember?"

"Yes, I do now . . . it was years ago . . . What's happened, the war's over?"

"I'm raising an expedition," Bradford said as they started through the woods back to Pemba's cabin.

"An expedition?" He was incredulous, and the remote expression left his face, replaced by bewilderment. "What do you mean?"

"We're going after the Yeti."

"Back to Everest?"

"No, he's been traced to Sierra."

"That's impossible," Pemba said. *"Foi ye!* How?"

"No one knows. Pemba, I want you to be my sirdar."

Pemba's eyes revealed shock and anxiety. It seemed

to Bradford that during this ten-year hibernation both of them had dreaded this moment. They had been imprisoned by their experience, and now the two survivors were being forced to be tested again.

Chapter Ten

It was late in the evening when the five men returned to the reservation. The Indian agent had been out on a bender for two days, and they took over his house for a preliminary strategy meeting.

The final member Bradford had selected for his team was a six-foot-five-inch Indian whom he had taught to climb when he first came to the reservation. Jamie Dask now spent part of the year as a guide, leading gentlemen mountaineers up scenic routes to Mount Whitney. He was an easy-going twenty-four-year-old who had hoped to play pro basketball. Although he was a strong rebounder for his size, he simply wasn't fast enough for the NBA.

Monte and Cathy were waiting for them. Monte had brought with him the scaled topographical map of Sierra and the layout of the resort. It was spread out on a rough-hewn rectangular table which was supported by wooden horses. For a while Monte watched with a sense of despair as Bradford moved a ruler and red felt pen over it, making crosses and triangles at various elevations. His fate was in the hands of this motley antisocial crew of wasted men. At best the prospects were bleak. He would lose the company money that had been advanced to Bradford and he would be eased out of his position. Word would get around to other companies, and Monte would be unemployable.

"The good news is that each man's share is fifty thousand dollars. An equal split," Bradford said as he studied his team's reactions. "The bad news is terrible. None of us is going to have the time to get into the condition we should be in for a high-altitude climb. You're not being paid that kind of money because we're going on a picnic. Some of us may die," he added, pitching his voice low so that the possibility gained a heightened reality. "If anyone has second thoughts, now's the time to pull out. When we're on the ice you may regret your decision."

Cathy watched him, and the pen trembled in her hand as she waited to list the supplies and equipment that would be required. He was courting death, challenging the other men to join him. Could such a man be stable? It was one thing to fight to protect one's life, but to climb onto the upper slopes of uncharted territory in sub-zero temperatures for the express purpose of encountering such a creature?

The unknown took on a form of unparalleled numbing shock as Bradford passed out the folder with the photographs of Janice's remains. The men examined the pictures impassively, as though they didn't believe them. Only Pemba understood what they meant. Bradford added other photos revealing the sheer face of the glacier and the giant towers of ice; these were even more grotesque than the dead girl, for they possessed the definite substance of actuality.

"What kind of animal did this?" Packard asked. The question started a tense murmuring among the men. Unless Bradford quickly squelched the super-human suggestions that were made, he knew, he'd lose them at the outset.

"It's a Snowman."

"We tracked him in the Himalayas," Pemba volunteered.

"How big?" Spider asked, studying the photograph.

"Larger than a bear," Bradford replied.

"Is he covered with fur?" Jamie inquired.

"The skin texture is something like a rhino's but it's covered by some kind of boned horns which protect it." They seemed to accept his explanation, without revealing any sign of fear.

"How much weight do we carry?" Jamie asked.

"What did you go up Whitney with?" Bradford inquired.

"Seventy-five pounds."

"At what altitude?" Pemba asked, running his finger along the route Bradford had traced.

"Thirteen thousand feet. We made a thousand feet an hour in snow."

"Well, we won't be able to come near that on an icefall," Bradford said with certainty. "I'd guess at base camp, which we'll pitch at about fifteen thousand feet, we might just manage fifty pounds a man. Cathy," he said, startling her, "you'll have to get in touch with Kelty's in L.A. and tell them I'll need the same kind of equipment they gave me before for a high-altitude climb on ice. We'll have to have snap-links, pitons, ice axes, Meade tents, sleeping bags, and primus stoves. We'll send them suit and boot sizes tomorrow, and I want them ready in a day. If they haven't got what we need, let them go to other retailers. All right, Monte?"

"Anything you say."

Spider moved toward the fire and stood there warming his hands. He was joined by Packard, who had filled two glasses with Jack Daniel's.

"For explosives I'd like to work with plastic cord," Spider said, sipping his drink. "M-79 grenade launchers, two flame throwers. Okay, Pack?"

"Carlos should have that in stock. It'll mean a trip to San Diego. An M-60 machine gun, which we can assemble and Jamie'll have to carry. If price is no problem, then I think each of us ought to have the Russian AK-47's."

"Carlos?" Monte interrupted.

"He arms all the mercenaries who come out of San Diego," Packard explained.

"Pity the 7.62 mini gun is too heavy. Fires seven thousand rounds a minute and nothing walks away from it," Spider said.

"It overheats," Packard said critically.

Spider lifted his glass to Bradford, but Bradford was shaking his head in disagreement. Packard asked, "What's the matter, Dan?"

"We can't use guns or explosives."

"I agree with Dan," Pemba said. "If you fire a pistol over a glacier we'll have an avalanche. There's no way you can risk firing!"

"Man, I was happy in jail. What the hell are you asking us to do, wear bedroom slippers and carry slingshots? Shit, I'm a demolitions expert, not a cat burglar," Spider said, downing his drink and furiously throwing the empty bottle against the cabin wall.

"Dan, for Christ's sake, we're going on trust with

you. Don't we have a right to protect ourselves?" Packard asked.

"He's got a point"—Jamie was on his feet, ill at ease and worried—"you're asking us to go into this blind and bare. That girl was ripped apart."

"They've got to have weapons," Monte insisted.

None of the protests, however, had any affect on Bradford. He seemed to have withdrawn into some inner world where he was beyond the plane of the nervous people surrounding him. They were now quarreling among themselves, attempting to come to terms with the suicide mission Bradford was luring them on. His eyes moved over each of the faces, a stare so disconcerting it forced them to turn away.

"Pack, set up a meeting with Carlos for tomorrow. I'll see you all in the morning."

Bradford left the cabin and walked into the sullen night. He was restless and concerned, grappling with a problem that had no logical solution. He strolled down to the stream and ran his hand in the cold, clear water. He lingered there for a few moments, listening to the rush of the stream as it thrust against the rocks, sending up cascades of fine spray. Nature has its music, and Bradford was attuned to it. He had deep regrets about leaving the reservation which had become his sanctuary.

Moving along the path was the lame figure of the Yaqui, an old man, bent and arthritic, leaning on a gnarled birch cane which one of the Indians had carved for him. The master and his disciple joined hands, but Bradford eventually withdrew his hand as though he had in some way betrayed the Yaqui.

"I don't think I'll be back," Bradford said.

"You can't know that."

"It's a feeling."

"Then don't go. Nothing is forcing you."

"The past is."

"There's no obligation to time. *La vida es sueño.* An illusion only, which innocent people try to define with clocks and calendars."

"The money I'm getting for this is going to the reservation for road equipment."

"Don't deceive yourself. It's not a question of helping the Indians that's driving you, but something personal."

Not grace but revenge, Bradford thought, was what continued to pursue him in those dark periods between sleeping and waking. He returned to his tent and squeezed the juice out of the mushroom the Yaqui had given him and swallowed it. The *Amanita muscaria* instantly brought with it wild dilating shapes. The book beside his camp bed was transformed into a bleeding head that sprang into the air and circled him like a bird of prey. He was transported back over the ice to the cave of the lamas and heard the singsong monody of holy men chanting as he lay on his stomach, his eyes unfocused and roving over the clumsy paintings of the Yeti and the miniature depictions of Oriental figures at the feet of the Snowman, their primitive bows aimed at the colossus. In his vision the arrows fired from the bows appeared as black specks, a swarm of insects which clung to the Snowman's chest.

Pemba held Bradford's head in the crook of his arm and tilted a chipped wooden bowl to his mouth. The sour taste of *rakshi,* the spirit the Nepalese distilled from rice, burned his throat. The alcohol went directly to his head, and he was by turns giddy and raving as the blurred images of the lamas stalked toward him. The painted devil masks concealed their faces, the prayer wheels spun, the melancholy sounds of the long trumpets buffeted his ears, and he heard his voice echo through the cave.

"I want to kill the Yeti! I'll kill—"

He did not recognize the woman who took hold of his hand, moved by his agony.

"It'll be all right, Dan. You've got friends," Cathy said, staring into the tormented eyes of this man who had seen what was forbidden to other human beings.

Chapter Eleven

When Carlos Millan picked the port of San Diego as the site of his warehouse, he recognized that he would have access to one of the greatest natural harbors in the world and that the nature of the city would allow him to remain anonymous. The city had the perfect climate for conspiracy.

The warehouse was a two-story structure with nothing to distinguish it from others lining the harbor. Built of wood, warped by the salt air, and with loose roof shingles blown by the wind coming from the sea, it gave no indication that it was a mere shell housing a large bunker—a bunker fitted with two-foot-thick stainless-steel doors guarded by a laser-beam alarm system—and that its floor could be tilted by a single switch located on Carlos's ornate Country French desk and the entire contents of the bunker dumped into the harbor in thirty seconds.

In order to get into Carlos's bunker Packard and Bradford went through metal detectors and were searched by bodyguards. Packard's photograph and fingerprints were checked in a data bank. Bradford reluctantly posed for his picture, was fingerprinted, and waited while an index file was begun under his name. No federal agents were going to walk in and bag Carlos unless they brought a battalion of Marines with them.

Carlos did not like references describing him as "in the gun or arms business." He saw himself as an armorer, a trade which possessed precedents of historical respectability. Although he sold guns which one of his factories secretly manufactured in Baja California, his profession was considerably more sophisticated. Carlos responded to challenges which would force him to use his ingenuity. He was an inventor, a specialist.

The difficulty of the problem presented to him by Packard and Bradford was just the kind that he enjoyed.

Bradford peered at the small, sallow-skinned man, whose otherworldly expression was that of a scholar who had spent years in a library, removed from the pleasures and concerns of everyday life. At every section of the bunker weapons were on display, placed on their crates for a buyer to examine: AK-70's, .50-caliber anti-aircraft guns, M-90 bazookas, 90mm mortars, M-69 grenade launchers, eight-foot-long recoilless rifles, and a single 50mm howitzer. It was an arsenal with the finest modern weapons used by the Army, and it would take just that kind of firepower to overpower Carlos and the thirty-odd men who worked for him.

"I don't see how I can help," Carlos said. He sipped a cup of yerba maté tea, then puffed on his cigar. "I'm fascinated, or perhaps 'tantalized' is the better word. How—*Madre de Dios*—do you propose to kill whatever it is you are after in the mountains without causing an explosion? Perhaps biological warfare or nerve gas?"

"No. Even if we could drop it over the area, we'd kill all the wildlife and innocent people."

Carlos turned to Packard. "Why don't the two of you work at something more reasonable? They could use you in Argentina or Rhodesia or any of the African nations who need mercenaries."

Bradford refrained from explaining the nature of his mission. How could he rationally describe the Yeti, the awesome power of the creature, without arousing Carlos's contempt? He took out a sheet of paper on which he'd made a rough drawing. He laid it on the desk.

"A bow?" Carlos said. It was difficult to know if he was jeering or simply surprised. "It never would have occurred to me."

"A crossbow with a telescopic sight."

Packard was irate, and in his anger he began to tremble with frustration. "Dan, I don't know what's wrong with you, but this is suicidal."

"Be patient," Carlos counseled, moving to a drawing board and turning on a high-intensity light. "Go on . . ."

"I'd need something light, a compound. Aluminum alloy constructed with pulleys and levers and a stabilizer."

"You'd get greater velocity and much flatter trajectory than with a recurve bow," Carlos said as he gracefully moved a drawing pencil over a fine sheet of paper.

"I'd need that because of wind factor. A hundred-pound compound would be like shooting a hundred-and-forty-pound recurve."

"With the levers and pulleys you'd increase the speed," Carlos noted approvingly. "And that would enable you to overcome the problem of decreased speed with a conventional bow because of the arching flight."

Bradford nodded and stood over Carlos's drawing board. He pointed to the trigger.

"If you could make an automatic trigger release, the cable could be held back indefinitely."

"I agree."

"What kind of material could be used for the cable?" he asked as Packard paced the bunker, stopping to examine heavy artillery and occasionally interrupting by calling out, "You fuckers are crazy."

"Aircraft cable," Carlos replied. "I can construct it so that it can be taken apart in three sections, the riser and two limbs. It will have pylons where the limbs and handle join, and there will be two pulleys for the wire aircraft cable. You'd be able to assemble it in five minutes."

"Pack, listen, will you? The compound crossbow we're talking about improves accuracy. The pull is easier, and the arrow strikes faster and with greater power."

"What would the maximum range be?" Packard asked, holding a bazooka.

"A hundred yards, I'd guess," Carlos replied.

"Well, how the hell are we going to hit it without a sight?"

Carlos turned to Bradford and smiled.

"That's easy. I'll mount a sniper's sight using a 100×100 Zeiss telescopic sight with a 210mm zoom."

"Sounds terrific," Packard said sarcastically. "And we fire arrows, I guess."

"That's right," Bradford insisted. "Stainless steel with razor-blade-sharp broadheads and fletched in red so that we can follow the flight in the snow."

"What do you want to penetrate?" Carlos asked, looking perplexed.

"Something stronger than a rhino's hide," Bradford answered.

"But then"—Carlos threw up his hands in a gesture of futility—"it's hopeless."

"There has to be a way to solve this," Bradford insisted. "We can't quit now." The bows and arrows of the hunters in the cave painting had been representational, he realized. Symbols of primitive men attempting to defend themselves against a force of nature that was invincible.

Carlos wiped the sweat from his brow with a crisp Irish linen handkerchief and poured another cup of the bitter green tea.

"If sound is the governing factor, you still come back to the basic problem you started with. You can't cause an explosion."

For ten years Bradford had withdrawn from society and its pressures because he regarded himself as an outcast. Now he couldn't be vanquished again, just when the opportunity to redeem himself had presented itself.

Carlos's lips were moving, and he glared at Bradford. "How many times do I have to repeat myself?"

"I'm sorry."

"Does the arrow have to pierce the target?"

"How else do you kill . . . ?"

"Just suppose the arrow doesn't penetrate the target?"

"No good."

"If the arrow stuck to the target?"

"Then what?" Packard asked, yawning.

"If the head of the arrow were made of some non-slip plastic that adhered to ice and instead of causing an explosion on contact it created just the opposite effect. The target would disintegrate and you could still achieve your purpose."

"Total destruction?" Bradford asked, filled with quixotic optimism.

"Yes, I'm talking about an *implosion*. Whatever the arrow hit and penetrated would fragment from within."

"What sort of material would you use?"

Carlos returned to his drawing board and drew a round-headed arrow with what resembled a suction cap.

"Plutonium. I'd make miniature nuclear warheads that would operate on transistors."

"Is it possible?"

"For a price, anything is possible."

"We'll need five crossbows and at least ten arrows per man."

"That's impossible. The plutonium source I have doesn't handle that amount of material."

"How many then?"

"I can't say now."

Bradford broke through the emotional barrier that controlled him and embraced Carlos.

"You make them and we'll pay."

Carlos, for his part, was reluctant to let Bradford leave. After a dinner invitation to his estate in La Hoya had been declined, his attitude became almost paternal.

"You're not going after a man, are you?"

"No. That'd be easy."

"Well, Dan, if you ever decide to go in for conventional assassination, I can put you in touch with a

South African group. They're offering a million dollars in any currency for Amin. I think it would be less dangerous than whatever you're going after."

When the party reached Los Angeles, Bradford noticed the enormous changes in the city during the years of his self-banishment. The smog was grittier and thicker, the freeways resembled giant snakes undulating with thousands of cars, and the sprawl of suburbia had manifested itself in cluster developments and high-rises. He had not missed much in the growth of civilization.

At Kelty's the men were fitted with Loewa double boots, thermal underwear, down parkas, sweaters, gloves, rain pants. Bradford selected mummy sleeping bags with ensolite pads because they were lighter than air mattresses. He and Pemba had always used Fritsch Himalaya ice axes and Mannut Swiss parallel 11mm nylon-strand-sheathed rope, the latter easy to follow or spot from the air because it was bright orange. Because the other men were not as experienced as they were, Bradford insisted, over Pemba's objections, on sixty-foot lengths, since they kinked less than the one twenty.

The tents and the rest of the heavy equipment were loaded on Monte's Lear jet. In late afternoon, when Bradford finally stepped aboard the plane, he was seized by a dizzying fit of anxiety. He was troubled by the possibility of what might happen to these men whom he liked; more than anything, he wanted them to be able to enjoy the money they were being paid.

There was still a good deal of grumbling about the weapon he and Carlos had devised. Would it actually work? When he explained why he had selected a bow, only Packard supported him. The others gave the impression that they might hold out until the last night before abandoning him. Even Pemba and he were becoming tense and antagonistic toward each other; he wondered whether the Sherpa who had once saved his life had now become snow-shy.

He told himself it didn't matter. If it came to it, he would go alone.

Chapter Twelve

The plane banked steeply through a web of dense clouds. Bradford was transfixed. The snow . . . he had thought he would never see it again. Glistening and forbidding, it possessed a mystery for him as inscrutable as the sea's. The attraction was so profound that he was shaken. He was a man who had been in exile. Now he had come home.

From the air he saw frozen alkali lakes. The mountain was made up of minarets and volcanic domes. Cirques, mosaiclike amphitheater-shaped bowls, formed giant pocks in the range.

The landing seemed to take forever. When he finally left the plane and felt the chill wind gust over the tarmac into his face, he embraced it like a lover. He felt the snow with his bare hands. The sense of complete peace that had eluded him during his wandering slowly returned. He was back in his element.

Intoxicated by the air, Bradford drove the large equipment-loaded truck with the window open. The men in the rear grumbled, but Pemba's good spirits had returned, and he was shouting, *"Sherpas Zindabad!"* Long live the Sherpas!· Even the crunch of the tire chains grating on the slick, icy road excited him.

As they approached the lodge the traffic increased, and they saw groups of colorfully dressed people carrying their skis along the steep embankment. Surrounding them were the high Sierras, their summit obscured by a haze of swirling frosted air.

Where would the Snowman be? Bradford visualized the giant form climbing over a layer of snow, bridging a crevasse as it scoured the mountain for prey.

He turned the truck into the driveway, and cinders splayed against the rear axle.

"It's not going to be an easy climb," Pemba said, his eyes narrowing, focusing on the terrain. But then he smiled and clasped Bradford's arm, moved by the challenge. They were climbers, and they had been away too long.

The team was staying in the ski instructors' building. To explain their presence, Bradford told them all to say they were engineers carrying out a survey for additional ski lifts. He asked the men to avoid getting involved with the guests while he and Pemba set out with maps and binoculars for a preliminary reconnaissance of the mountain.

From her office Cathy watched him fixing the bindings on his two-meter Rossignol skis. He crouched low and pushed off in fluid thrusts, moving like a powerful engine. For the first time since she had met him, Bradford seemed truly happy. He and Pemba got on the ski lift and were soon out of sight. She returned to her work, thinking of him, unable to still the strange excitement he aroused in her.

From the lift, Bradford and Pemba scanned the

mountain for signs of tracks. Neither of them knew at what altitude the Snowman would descend. They had encountered him at twenty-eight thousand feet, but the attack on the girl had occurred at roughly half that altitude. The slopes were filled with skiers of all ages; they'd be defenseless if the Snowman attacked.

At the experts' slope they skied off the lift and went into the hut, where the man awaiting them showed them where to store their skis and change to their boots and crampons. Pemba was wearing his old parka with the Tiger badge awarded him by the Himalayan Club for climbing proficiency. The man in the hut stared at Pemba with a mixture of curiosity and respect. It was obvious to Bradford that he had never seen a Sherpa. But when the man asked where they were from, Bradford simply ignored the question and set out with Pemba for the first climb.

The thin, rarefied air slowed them as they kick-stepped above the hut. Their boots were stiff, and the prongs of the crampons slashed into the icy slope. When they had advanced some four hundred feet, they stopped and noted a col, a depression in the mountain chain that they could use as a mark when the full party made the ascent. Just above them a snout appeared, the lower terminus of the glacier. It was the bluish-green color that came from melting during the summer months before the freeze with the first snows.

"It will go," Bradford said, indicating that the terrain was passable.

"The south ridge might be the best way of attack if we have to go up to the summit," Pemba said, speaking slowly to conserve his energy. In the past a climb at this altitude would have been simple for him, but now he was out of condition.

"Cornices below it . . . to the west it looks tricky. Could be snow bridges, so we better avoid it," Bradford replied, even though the alternative was a treacherous climb into the prevailing wind. At this altitude wind was the constant, relentless enemy.

The glacier was large, magnificently angled, and so steep that the force of gravity which created it allowed the snow to move downhill. To Bradford each new glacier was an uncharted river which he, the explorer, must study, learning its drops in elevation, its rises, the speed at which it moved. Where the change was precipitous, the glacier always contained a mass of fissures which were as dangerous as the rapids in an unnavigable river. Fortunately, they were not now near water. Once, in a climb on the Humboldt Glacier in Greenland, he had almost been killed when a section of it had shattered, *calved*, and a great mountain had joined the other monolithic icebergs floating in the sea around it.

They climbed another two hundred feet and were confronted by a gigantic icefall. The frozen cascade of ice was not on their map. It had been formed when the glacier had changed direction in the slope of the ground beneath it.

"It's a fucker," Bradford said.

"We'll have to make base camp below it," Pemba agreed. This would increase their hardship if they had to reach the summit, since their camp would be thousands of feet below it. They would have to cross the icefall horizontally, perhaps even diagonally higher up; this traverse would use up vital time and deplete their energy.

On the climb back down to the hut they carefully followed the platforms made by their kick-steps earlier.

The afternoon light was still good. When they changed back to skis, Bradford led Pemba down to the place where Janice had been found. He still skied magnificently, but he knew that time had warped his skills; the driving power required for a giant slalom, whipping past the gates at fifty miles an hour, was now beyond him. The fluid grace was still present, but that inner rhythm had been lost. The two men threaded their way through a cordoned path of whitebark pines off the main ski run; the slopes had thinned out considerably since they had gone up. Occasionally Bradford caught a blurred glimpse of a solitary figure getting in a final run for the day.

The snow along the path was mixed with gray spikes of frozen rock. They continued to search for tracks, even though they were losing the light. As they skied along the cross-country trail, loose snow constantly blew in a spatter from the tree branches. When they reached a clearing in the woods, they saw a trail of frozen blood and beyond it huge triangular indentations pocking the ice. Pemba said, *"Husiar"*—be careful. Then he fell silent, mesmerized by the sight. The soft cast of his face seemed as lifeless as a mask.

Bradford's past flight flooded back, and he trembled. Somehow he had to overcome his fear. He had spent years dreaming about the Yeti, but now, faced with the possibility that an encounter might occur at any time, he began to lose his resolve. Panic would be contagious. He forced himself to examine the tracks. He took off his gloves and touched the blackened ground formed by the tracks.

"It's petrified," he said. "The heat he gives off must burn right through the ice . . . down to the rock layer. When the tracks are new they're rainbow-colored."

He managed to gain control of himself, and realized that his fears stemmed from the fact that he was unarmed. Pemba shied away down the side of the trail and signaled him to move. Yet Bradford stood his ground. The ecstacy of mindless blood lust overwhelmed him. For now, at least, he too was a savage.

Monte's office was expensively paneled in tongue-and-groove cedar, but one wall was made entirely of glass with sliding doors; it commanded a magnificent view of the slopes, now illuminated in the full moon. Bradford stood watching the mountain. He had a Scotch in his hand, which he sipped almost absent-mindedly. He anticipated some movement, but all he was able to see were the long shroudlike shadows cast by the cliff line. The sky was candescently clear, and outside the window lovers kissed under the stars, unaware of the dangers thousands of feet above.

"The smartest thing you could do would be to close down," he said.

"Listen, I'm not totally crazy," Monte replied indignantly. He turned to Cathy. "Our sales are taking off and he wants me to chase the buyers."

Monte's ferret face registered disapproval, and in his small blue eyes there was that shady glint of a shopkeeper's avarice.

"Monte, we're up against something completely unpredictable. From the tracks I saw today, I know the Snowman's prowling."

"I don't like to take sides, Dan, but I think Monte's got a point. There's more than nine hundred people up," Ashby said. "You'd have to mount an evacuation. People'd start talking . . . On the other hand, they

126

could stay and draw even larger crowds if they think they're going to see something."

"If we were to close the slopes, what would you expect the people to do?" Cathy asked.

"They could stay indoors and screw for all I care. I just don't like it."

Ashby sensed trouble. Any unusual restrictions would be certain to draw outside attention to Sierra. Stringers on some of the major papers as well as human-interest TV reporters might be alerted.

"Fact is, there's been no attack or even a sighting since he killed the girl," Ashby said in support of Monte.

"Jim, I saw a trail of frozen blood in the pine forest."

"Could've been anything . . . an animal." Ashby poured him another drink. Bradford had to be handled delicately, and Ashby joined whichever side afforded him the most protection. He'd already written five thousand words on Janice, but he realized that, apart from the facts provided by Bradford, most of the material could be dismissed as speculation. He needed the buttress of a visual sighting, photographs, or, better yet, the dead Snowman to support his story.

"I think it might help if you spoke to the young man who saw Janice last. He might have noticed some detail that would mean something to you," Ashby continued. "Monte fixed it. He's waiting in the bar for you."

Cathy picked up the signal, and she remembered what Ashby had told her earlier in the day:

"I'm not anybody's enemy, honey, just my own best friend." He had proved his case.

She put on her parka and with Bradford in tow left the office. She was glad to be alone with him finally,

even though he seemed to calculate emotional invest-
ments with the care of an orphan's guardian. He gave
very little of himself.

The slopes were like black steel knifeblades in the
moonlight. They were no longer, and never again
would be, the innocent runs of the past. They had
a texture of something malevolent, forbidden, and a
chill ran through her as they made their way through
the crowded lobby to the bar.

At a table in the corner she spotted Barry and
threaded her way to him through an aisle of ski-bunny
waitresses whose trays were slopped with pitchers of
beer. Bradford stood awkwardly, as though inhibited
by the sight of the crush of people. He nodded formally
when she made the introductions.

"Christ, it scares me to think of this bunch skiing,"
Bradford said.

"Monte just needs a few more bodies to make him
change his mind," Barry said, sullen and red-eyed
with booze.

"You were with the girl when she was attacked,
weren't you?" Bradford said.

There was a burned expression on Barry's face, of
an indelible memory, which Bradford recognized. He
had seen it on his own face for years.

"I should've been. I never left a beginner before—"

"It happens. Did you notice anything odd or hear
something before you left her?"

Barry leaned back on his chair, gripping his drink
tightly.

"No, not really. It started to snow, which is hardly
unusual up here. Nothing else." He paused for a moment and tried to control himself, but the strain was
too great. "I can't get her face out of my mind—"

"Barry—" Cathy interrupted, sharing his distress.

"Her face. She was eaten! I mean, it was like a cannibal had—"

"I know," Bradford said.

"How could you possibly know?"

"I saw the photographs."

"Man, maybe you know about world-class skiing, but you don't know shit about what went on up there."

"Get it all out," Bradford said. "It's eating your guts."

Barry stared at him. "I'm afraid—I mean, just the thought of being up there on the slopes makes me panic. I watch the chairlift on seven every day and I know that I'll never be able to get on. It's all I can do to take a group up the poma on the ski-school slope. I've been getting headaches and vertigo. I see a girl's face and it's suddenly transformed into Janice's. I hear her voice, crying, accusing me. I deserted her. God, when I think of how much fun this used to be, I could cry. It's a life for chosen people, and you last until you're thirty, maybe; then you have to grow up and find something to do in the real world. But I'm finished at twenty-three. I've been skiing all my life, and there's nothing else I can do."

To Bradford, it was like listening to a voice from his own past. When he had tried to explain what had occurred to the skeptical members of the Explorers Club, he had suffered an anguish so fine that he himself had wondered about the accuracy of his own account. It was impossible even now to communicate the dread that had afflicted him. He felt a curious kinship with Barry. But Barry had not been attacked, had not seen the monstrosity towering over the mountain, ripping the flesh out of men, his mouth dripping blood as his teeth gnashed bone.

They fell silent, and a waitress brought them another round of drinks.

"You'll get your confidence back eventually," Bradford said, hoping he was right.

"Really? I was going to the Olympic tryouts in Sun Valley later this winter. I can't now, I'm unstrung," he said without self-pity. "I've got time to practice, but all I do is sit around and get bombed."

"It happened to me at the Olympics. I missed a gate on two practice runs and I knew that when I was in the shoot for real I'd have trouble. I got psyched."

"You won a bronze," Barry reminded him.

Bradford threw his head back and laughed raucously.

"Since when does finishing third get you brownie points? At times I can't believe that I even skied. It's all so long ago. When you're busted out in South America or wherever, a bronze medal doesn't get you a drink on the house."

"What brought you up here?" Barry asked.

"I used to climb as well. A lot better than I skied. And Cathy talked me into coming up as her guest for Thanksgiving."

"Climbing on ice?" Barry was incredulous.

"Uh-huh."

"But what does that have to do with what happened to the girl?" Barry persisted.

"I'm going to climb above the experts' slope with a team."

"To do what?"

"Find out if I can who or what killed Janice Pace." He extended his hand, then patted Barry on the shoulder. "This isn't general information, so don't discuss me with the other instructors or guests, Tiger."

"The temperature's forty below zero up there, and the summit is eighteen thousand feet."

"So I heard."

"It's an animal of some kind that we don't know about, isn't it?" Barry said.

"New strain of bear, maybe. I'll let you know. Now why don't you haul your ass into a sauna and hit the slopes early tomorrow morning and get yourself into shape?"

"Do you want to take a few runs with me?"

"I'd fall on my can. You guys are too good for me. I'd need a snowmobile to keep up with you."

"Come on, Dan."

"Another time." As he was about to leave, he could not restrain his curiosity. "What do you ski?"

"Two point three Rossies."

"I hear they're leaning back now on the downhill."

"Better balance and traction," Barry explained.

He turned to Cathy and said with resignation: "Everything changes."

Chapter Thirteen

Cathy's town house, which was just beyond the furnished models, had a sense of permanence. In the central living room there were books on the shelves, old family snapshots on the walls, and a rug which she had woven herself. The furniture appeared to have been acquired over a period of time: an antique desk, a low coffee table with a brass brazier holding a sprawling philodendron, a pair of brass lamps on the end tables. Large multicolored cushions were arranged around the fire. The cathedral ceiling and the stone fireplace the height of the wall gave Bradford a feeling of space.

It was good to see how she lived, for she now had an individuality that he had overlooked because his nightmare had reemerged. She was a warm, vulnerable woman, but married to a job she didn't quite belong in. He respected her independence yet wondered what sacrifices she'd been forced to make to secure it. Her attractiveness had been masked by a high-powered business persona, and he thought he would like to take off

133

her clothes slowly, deliberately, and touch her body. Cathy's energy was a disguise which he was determined to expose. It occurred to him that he might never again have an opportunity to make love. He reminded himself of a soldier going off to war who on his last night's leave had met a girl who'd carry him through the bad times.

She went into the bedroom to change her clothes. "What do you do for women on the reservation?" she asked through the partially opened door.

"Pick one for the night. What about men for you?"

"I'm still recovering from the last one. I was engaged to a married man, if such a relationship can exist."

"What happened?"

"His lawyer advised him that he'd be better off staying married. It came down to keeping his net worth or starting again with me, so here I am," she said, coming out of the bathroom and throwing her arms out in a theatrical gesture which made him smile. She was wearing blue suede pants and a light pink turtleneck sweater. She put on a pair of dark gray après-ski boots.

"You don't sound very wounded."

"It's my poker face. And it's a damned useful story when any of the men up here come on too strong. The male ego is pathetically fragile, and guys quit fast when they're told that you're still in love with someone else."

He laughed. "Which brings us back to what *do* you do?"

He held her jacket for her and breathed in the soft fragrance of her hair.

"I hang in tough until I meet a beautiful crazy like you."

He kissed her lightly on the lips and said: "Good."

He walked with his arm around her up to the lodge, and before she moved off they stood looking up at the mountain, desolate in the cold night air. Music and loud voices drifted out from the lodge. She tightened her grip on his arm, but he was gone from her again. He grimaced as though in the throes of pain that he could not communicate.

He left her beside a high snowdrift and began walking up the slope. She called to him, but he didn't respond and so she went alone into the lobby. The gusts of hot air from the heater made her flush and created a spiky sensation on her cheeks. She hung up her parka on a peg and went to the window to look for him. She thought she saw a man's shadow above the ski school, but then it was gone. She had already lost Bradford; only the thought of him remained, elusive and puzzling like an undefined foreboding.

A band of bored mischievous kids rushed through the lobby. They were led by a scrawny, loutish, thick-lipped boy who stuck his tongue out to her, then puckered his mouth and made a farting sound. But she was not his target. He rushed through the musicians and slammed the keys of the piano to interrupt them. When a few adults objected, he darted past them toward the game room.

A frustrated woman shouted: "Willie, you cut that out now!" A heavy-set man with an unkempt beard chided the woman.

Fascinated by the monstrous boy, Cathy poked her head into the game room. The children's entertainment consisted of a nightmare collection of gun games, pinball machines, miniature bowling lanes, pool tables where unskilled boys clawed the felt with unchalked cues. Willie was at the change machine, surrounded by his entourage. He kicked the machine and shouted "Gyp!" His anger spent, he opened a small toolkit attached to his Western belt and removed a long, thin dental-type instrument and proceeded to pick the lock. He removed a stack of dollar bills and pocketed most of them, then distributed a single to each of the kids and said: "Hush money. If anyone squeals—girls or not—I'll kick their ass in."

The bully and the thief were consummated in perfect union. She walked away in disgust. But the sea of adult faces around her was no improvement. The adults gathered around the lottery counter, where tickets were being distributed by ski instructors. A heightened expression of greed marked them all, like stamps from a machine. What, she asked herself, was she doing in this place? Free house or not, she wasn't equipped to handle these people week after week. Their problems, children, drunkenness, the clumsy sexual innuendoes of dull men and the plaintive voices of submissive women were too much.

"Life's too damned short," she told herself, making her way to the table, where a large glass barrel was mounted on metal staves. She picked up a microphone and addressed the crowd.

"Ladies and gentlemen, welcome to Great Northern Lodge. In five minutes we're going to have the drawing for our magnificent, completely furnished Chamonix town home. Those of you who haven't got a ticket, please go up to the ski desk, where you'll be given one. May I remind you that it's one ticket per family. Thank you."

Her voice sounded like a whining electric guitar over the tinny P.A. system.

She worked her way into the bar and managed to get a drink at the service hatch.

A large map was spread over Monte's glass desk. Bradford pointed to a series of routes he had chartered earlier in the day to correct topographical and ordinance errors.

The men surrounded him. The drinks Monte had furnished were beginning to loosen them up. At least only Bradford and Pemba had any inkling of what they could expect once the climb began. As he looked at the faces around the table, he observed an air of security, which the circumstances hardly justified. Yet he realized that if he were to behave cautiously, the mood would change and the men might again begin to balk.

"We'll be able to move our equipment up on the gondola tomorrow morning and we'll make base camp at this point. There's a col running across here, and we'll need a couple of days to find the best site."

"Are we going up to the summit?" Jamie asked.

"Not if we can help it," Pemba answered. "We located the contour line of the glacier, and there're bound to be cleavages running along it."

"What's the approximate angle?" Packard asked, leaning over the map.

"About sixty degrees at the snout, which means that it'll become more acute—possibly thirty degrees—at the top, where it'll form a bowl." Bradford ran his pen along the glacier line. "Once we get over the bowl the mountain'll be too steep to contain the glacier. We'll encounter bergschrunds beyond, because stationary snowfields have to form at the terminus of a glacier. How wide they'll be is anybody's guess. On the Khumbu glacier in the Himalayas they sometimes run a city block and we had to go around them, which meant a longer climb. But there's no reason to anticipate anything of that size. Still, we'll have to be on our guard for concealed moats when we pass the schrunds. They can stretch as far down as the glacier snout."

Monte abruptly asked: "When do you think you can start?"

"Aren't you getting your money's worth, boss?" Spider asked.

"What the hell do you think we're doing?" Jamie, usually reserved, burst out. "Man, you don't just start up a mountain in midwinter without planning. Once we're up there, we've got more than any monster to worry about. One careless step and it's over for us."

The phone rang. Monte picked it up and said to Bradford, "Carlos, for you."

Bradford listened attentively, and when he frowned, the men began to talk nervously among themselves.

"No, we can't wait till next week. We can't move until you've delivered them." He held the receiver and turned to Monte. "Can you send your plane to San Diego for him?" Monte nodded. "Ten o'clock."

"What's the matter?" Packard asked.

"That's my problem," Bradford said brusquely.

The air of secrecy disturbed them, and Bradford knew he had lost their attention. He recognized the signs of jitters.

"Dan, are you holding out on us?" Spider insisted. "Shit, man, if we're in trouble already we ought to know about it."

"Let me do the worrying."

"When it's my ass, I've got a right to be concerned," Packard said. "Fact is"—he huddled with Spider—"these bows'll never work. You couldn't hunt deer with them."

"Any time you want to get back to your ranch, just say the word and you're on your way."

Packard lurched drunkenly toward him.

"Don't make me drop you, Pack."

Spider pulled him away and the two of them returned to the bottle of Jack Daniel's.

This bunch had grown wobbly before they'd started. In a dangerous situation on the face of the mountain, when the leader's word was law, they might panic and turn on him. He had to do something to pull them together.

"Listen, the two of you fought in one of the dirtiest wars—"

"Right!" Packard slammed the table. "The politicians fucked us around. We were numbers. Garbage that no one gave a whore's twat for. And we don't want to go through the same thing again. Don't you understand? Sure, we all need the money—and we want it, goddamn it. But the deeper we get sucked in, the less we know. Thing was, you were somebody I believed wouldn't buddy-fuck me, but Christ almighty, you spook us, Dan. Why are you doing this? What's in it for you?" He flung the bottle of Jack Daniel's into the fire, and it exploded like a bomb, throwing off shards of glass around the room.

"I don't want to die either, and I care about all of you," Bradford said quietly. "I was attacked by the Snowman and I lost my whole party."

"How many?" Spider asked, as though the number

of casualties would provide him with a touchstone by which to measure his own chances of survival.

"Nineteen," Pemba said regretfully. "Only Dan and I got away."

Unexpectedly, Packard began to laugh, a crazy high-pitched squall.

"Numbers," he said again. "We had lost most of our brigade by the time we got to Cambodia. But at least we had the satisfaction of fragging plenty of dinks along the way."

"How many were kids?"

"I lost count," Packard said indifferently. "When somebody points a gun at me, I don't ask for a birth certificate."

Bradford turned to Spider. "Would *you* do it again?"

"Sure," Spider said. "I believed in what it was about when I enlisted. And after all the friends I lost, I'd go back."

"Well, maybe my reasons won't be so hard to understand. How many times in a lifetime do you get a chance for revenge? This is my shot."

Chapter Fourteen

While the drawing was in progress, Willie led the group of children through the deserted kitchen. Cooling on the counters were dozens of turkeys which were to be served at the free lunch the lodge was providing its potential customers for Thanksgiving. He located a large plastic bag, seized a whole bird, and carried it out the back door.

"We're going to have a picnic in the sky," he announced grandly. "Anyone who wants a taste has to come with me."

The children, thrilled by his craft and sheer audacity, excitedly agreed. They found their parkas in the lobby and joined their leader outside.

"Where're we going?" a young girl asked.

"For a ride."

A fine, powdery snow was falling. On the way the boys packed snowballs and threw them wildly at cars. A sense of elation and release from parental restrictions spread through the five boys and three girls.

Julie, a nine-year-old, fell back with Lori, her ten-year-old friend.

"He's crazy," Julie said.

"But isn't it fun?" Lori said, running a few steps for fear of being left behind.

They followed Willie blindly as he glissaded on slick downhill patches of ice. When they reached the gondola shed he switched on the light and said, "Now let's see how this damn thing works."

A plump boy wearing a hat with earmuffs under his parka hood said, "I always wanted to be an engineer."

In the lodge the musicians were playing nerve-rending chords on their electric guitars and Cathy was calling for quiet. When she had the attention of the mob, she placed her hand on the drum.

"The winner of Great Northern's drawing will receive our Chamonix town home, which has one bedroom and a loft. It is valued at thirty-nine thousand nine hundred and ninety-nine dollars. Your chalet will be completely furnished by Rose's Interiors of Sierra." She waited as a buzz of expectation rippled through the crowd. Women clutched their tickets and gazed lovingly at their husbands.

Cathy spotted Bradford at the back of the room, surrounded by his group of men. She spun the barrel.

It was just a matter of turning the power switch, nothing more complicated than that, Willie discovered as the engine plant in the gondola shed roared into life. Greased pulleys turned on metal belts, and the cable on an overhead T-track moved the gondolas as though they were robots. The children jammed into a single car, and Willie brushed up against Julie. They were all giggling and shouting.

"Keep quiet till we move past the lodge," Willie ordered them. "Sound carries, and we don't want to get caught."

The gondola moved sluggishly over the ski-school slope, and the children pressed against the glass as the lights below became dim and opaque. Moving higher, the car began to sway in a crosscurrent of wind. Julie noticed that the snow was heavier. It lashed the window, and whining eerie noises troubled her.

In the back of the car, Willie put the turkey on a seat and started to tear the bird apart.

Cathy put her hand into the barrel, and there were nervous shouts and moans from women who encircled her. She picked up a ticket.

"The winner is the William Stevenson family! Congratulations!"

The bearded man and his red-nosed wife snuffling into a ragged Kleenex burst through the crowd. The man hollered, "That's us!"

"Willie, where's Willie?" the woman cried out. "Wait'll he hears!"

It had to be this pair who won, Cathy thought, remembering the monstrous boy they had brought forth. She smiled, and was forcibly kissed by both when she presented the keys to the condo. A table had been reserved in the bar for the winners, and Monte ordered champagne for them. She found herself carried along, unable to break away and join Bradford and his men at a corner of the bar.

* * *

The gondola passed over the beginners' slope and was now three thousand four hundred and eighty-one feet up the mountain. It shuddered from side to side. The snowfall was heavier as it moved higher. Inside the children huddled in a corner, unable to stand up. The wind velocity increased, lashing the car. Thick granules of sleet caromed off the windows like machine-gun fire, and Julie whispered tearfully to her friend, "We're going to die." The floor of the car was littered with turkey bones, and the carcass and greasy skin made her sick to her stomach.

"I'm scared," one of the boys said.

"Well, if you want to get off, chicken, don't let me stop you," Willie replied angrily. He too was frightened by the shaking cable, but he was determined to bluff it out. "Ladies and gentlemen, we're experiencing some temporary turbulence. Please fasten your seat belts and extinguish all cigarettes."

"You're horrible," Lori said. "This is crazy."

No one contradicted her, and she peered out of the fogged window. She blew on it, then wiped it with the back of her glove. They were above a pine forest. The trees were so high that the gondola seemed to skirt over their branches. The snow below was blinding. Caught in the insurgent eddying winds, it thrashed the forest.

"Something's moving on the mountain!" Lori shouted tearfully. It was gone as soon as she spoke.

"Next time stay home and play with your dolls," Willie said.

The temperature inside had dropped to ten below zero, and when Lori rubbed her eyes she discovered that her tears were frozen to the lashes and her face was becoming numb. She began to breath rapidly, and she thought her lungs would explode. She heard some of the boys sobbing in the back of the car.

Following the gondola on the intermediate slope was the Snowman. The car moved slower than he did, but it changed direction unexpectedly. His hand flailed the air, slashing across the trunks of heavy pines and felling them. The mountainside was littered with trees. He slithered across a giant mogul, then waited for the object to pass within his reach.

"Hey, there's a light on the mountain," Willie said, startled.

"You're nuts," one of the boys cheeped weakly. He staggered to the rear window.

"It's a lighthouse beam," Willie insisted, pointing at the image. But then the light was gone, and he wondered if it had been his imagination, or perhaps the light of the moon reflecting off the ice. There was a thunderous sound of ice smashing, and a huge block flew past the window. Willie was now too terrified to speak, and he sank to the floor, howling, infantile, and without hope. All around him the children he had led on this insane expedition gasped for breath and writhed as though stricken by some poison gas.

A sharp reverberating whine which sounded like some form of giant cat was heard. The children began to scream. Julie struggled to her feet. She was stepping on a body. The gondola was nearing the experts' run, and through the gales of snow there were brief intervals of visibility when the wind knifed through, dividing the snow into a series of unsupported walls. A large shadow loomed beneath them. Her stomach turned, and her chest was on fire as her body throbbed in short spasms of dry heaves. The cat sound now mysteriously turned into a frenzied roar which echoed through the mountain depression. She sank once again to the floor.

It's following us, she thought, powerless to move.

The cable of the gondola was jarred, and the vibrations shook the car. The children, mute with terror, came to life again and broke into a gagging dirge. The gondola started its descent, breaking into snarling headwinds which struck it with the force of a hammer.

The Snowman groped along a narrow arête. The ridge caved in, and he lost his balance. He dug into the side of an ice chimney; his claws gave him the traction to right himself. He saw the moving black line, and he stretched up once again to tear at it. A blanket of snow covered him, and he hacked at the icefall, fracturing a large mass; then he descended into the sérac below him.

"Finally . . . I thought this circus would never end," Cathy said. She and Bradford walked arm in arm down past the lodge.

He stopped and turned his head, and she leaned her head on his shoulder, expecting him to kiss her. The new snow was falling heavily, but the moon was not obscured at ground level.

"Do you hear that?"

It was a faint whirring of machinery.

"Could be a car turning over."

"No, it's a lift."

They jogged toward the T-bars, which were closer than the lifts or gondolas.

"Are they crazy, using the gondolas at night?"

Above them empty cars rattled on the overhead track.

"Maybe they're being tested."

"Not in this wind. They can be derailed."

They climbed the steps into the shed. The lights were on, and the pulleys rotated smoothly.

"Can I borrow your lipstick?"

Puzzled, she reached into her bag and found it.

"What're you going to do?"

He marked an X across a gondola about to leave the platform.

"If this one comes down again we'll know nobody's inside any of the others," he explained. "Otherwise, if I switch off the power someone might be trapped in one."

They waited apprehensively as a number of empty cars passed them. Somewhere outside the shed there was a gabble of voices carried by the wind. It grew closer, and now the sounds were shrieks of panic. The gondola reached them, and Bradford opened the door. The children were massed on the floor, crying and groaning. Cathy and Willie exchanged an angry look; then the boy lowered his eyes and began to bawl.

"Whose crazy idea was this?" Bradford asked.

Cathy knew there was no need for an answer. She pulled Willie out onto the platform. "Is there anybody else up there?"

"No . . . just us."

They escorted the children back to the lodge, to be claimed by their parents. Willie said in a faltering voice, "There's something up there. The girls saw it too."

"Forget it," Bradford said. "Probably your imagination. You were all pretty scared."

"It was gigantic. It made sounds like a cat, but it wasn't a cat . . ."

* * *

Bradford sat with Cathy in her living room, staring at the fire and drinking brandy. He was relieved that the children were safe. They had accused Willie of instigating the trouble, but his parents, overwhelmed by winning the condominium, had taken the easy way out and let him off with a reprimand.

Outside the wind had gained momentum, and thrashed the loose snow from the drifts. Standing by the window, Cathy watched the snow pummeling against the warming hut at the base of the slopes.

"We can use the snow."

"Hasn't it been snowing regularly?" he asked, looking up with some surprise.

"No, it's the damnedest thing. We usually get one of the highest snowfalls in the States. But this year the weather's been so peculiar."

"In what way?"

"The way it starts, then peters out. In the past, once it began we'd have snow every day."

"When was the last time it snowed?"

"The afternoon Janice was killed."

Bradford pondered the implications, then went to refill his glass. He stood by the mantelpiece, trying to make some sense out of the circumstances.

"It was snowing when I was attacked. It never occurred to me to make a connection. The Snowman comes out when it's snowing. He was on the mountain tonight. I know it. The kids saw him. But why when it snows? Does it have something to do with the food supply or the ice movement?" he asked rhetorically. "Or possibly sound? When I was on Lhotse with my party, our electronic equipment went haywire, and we thought it might have been the weather conditions or the altitude. But during that entire period we kept

148

hearing an ultra-high-pitched sound which echoed on the mountains, and I was sure that it was wind trapped in an ice chimney."

She drew the curtains and moved to the fireplace. She sat on the rug, removed her boots and socks, and warmed her feet by the fire.

"It's a full-blown blizzard out there," she said, chilled and shuddering. "Dan, when you followed after Hillary, you must have had some theories about the Snowman."

"They were considered too unscientific for publication, which is why I had to go out and try to find some evidence to support my ideas. A lot of good it did me," he added angrily. "Christ, we were so badly organized, and our camera equipment froze. There just wasn't enough money to mount a proper expedition."

"How do you think the Snowman evolved?"

"I don't know . . . the Snowman is nature's ultimate survivor. The sheer weight and size of him is beyond belief. He could take a great white shark and rip its head off and eat it the way we polish off an apple. Cathy, I saw him with my own eyes. He just lashed out and hacked a sérac off the mountain. The power he has is beyond comprehension. Hundreds of tons of ice were just mashed into a pulp."

"But how could he possibly get here, to the high Sierras?"

"He probably lost his food supply in the Himalayas and had to find the right climatic conditions. He may have lived here for years, preying on the wildlife, before there was any resort here."

She had again lost Bradford. His eyes were glazed, and he seemed drugged or hypnotized by the idea of his quest. She wrapped her arms around him, terrified by the drive which haunted him, but he seemed not to feel her.

"The lamas call him *Sogpa,*" he said finally. "Satan."

They had gone into the bedroom together without either a signal or any discussion. It just seemed the natural thing to do.

"I don't remember the last time I was in a woman's bedroom," he said.

He lifted up her pale pink ski skivvy. Her breasts were firm and warm and he unclasped the bra hook in front, exposing them. He stroked them with his fingertips and then kissed her. She had expected something else, something to match the violence he seemed to contain, not this wonderfully gentle caressing.

She realized that she was crying soundlessly when he removed her pants. In a moment they were both under the covers, naked. He brushed the tears away with his index finger, then tasted them with his tongue. He pressed against her, and she felt him stubbornly force himself inside. He was growing larger inside her, exploring her. She arched her back and let him thrust deeper.

He remained inside her for most of the night, and she felt herself come even as she dozed. It was still dark—perhaps four in the morning—when she touched his shoulder-length hair. She remained awake the rest of the night, convinced that this was all she would have to remember. He was going to die, and there was nothing she could do about it.

She made a pot of coffee at about six and sat quietly before the window. The snow had stopped during the night, and she watched the bleak sky gradually lighten. The tortuous long icicles hanging from the window seemed threatening and dangerous. She was overcome by a depressing realization that she might never again see the man asleep in her bed. Her life was filled with these vicious, tantalizing surprises, which reached that gorgeous high point and then collapsed. Once again, she knew, she would be powerless to alter the course of events.

He would resent any plea to give up the climb. He was a man with a destructive purpose, charting the means and method of his own death. She and her company joined him in this collusion. All she would have from Bradford was one night.

"How can I hold him?" she asked herself, pouring another cup of coffee and studying the mountain peaks which were slowly defined by the shifting light—naked and jagged, coated with ice and pinnacles of treachery. She raised her fist at them in a futile gesture of rage.

"I don't want you to go up there," she said when he came out of the bedroom, tousle-haired, boyish, with a sheepish smile on his face.

He stroked her face, and she pulled away like an unyielding child punishing a contrite parent. But she knew her helplessness had no affect on him. He would not console her or try to convince her that he had to go. There would be no scene, no drama, just a friendly wave.

Which was precisely what occurred after they had finished breakfast. He kissed her, offered no good-bye, and, like some magician's illusion, he vanished. She cried during her bath, then dressed, put on her make-up, and tried to forget what was happening to her.

Chapter Fifteen

The team of men shifted their equipment to the gondola at seven. The lifts would not be opened to the public until eight thirty, so they would have ample time to reach the experts' slope. They would then begin the climb and make a start at establishing base camp. Ashby took Bradford aside and handed him a lightweight 35mm Nikon.

"As soon as you set up camp, let me know. Good luck."

The air was so dry that their nostrils burned; Bradford checked the oxygen equipment. He'd picked light alloy dural cylinders, which weighed eighteen pounds. A USAF mask used by pilots of F111 jets was fitted with inlet valves; an economizer enabled each man to control his own mixture. A spirit of camaraderie took hold of them now that they were on the mountain. The bickering of the previous night was forgotten. Much of the new snow had frozen overnight, but there were still dangerous areas of soft powder which had built up in drifts over fifteen feet high.

Bradford, carrying sixty pounds of equipment in a backpack, led the party up to the icefall. The twelve-point Grivel crampons they wore enabled them to slash through the different textures of ice and snow. The drop was not precipitous, and there was no need to climb belayed with rope. If anyone fell he could stop by self-arrest or glissading. The morning was clear, and from his position at the head Bradford could make out the line of the summit. It was surrounded by groups of sharply angled cornices. Below them, encircling the summit and creating another barrier, was an immense depression.

At fourteen thousand, two hundred feet the temperature was sixteen below. It had dropped four degrees for each thousand-foot increase in elevation. The prevailing wind was southeast at ten knots, but this could change unexpectedly. They reached the icefall. In the luminous sun it spread out in an infinite gleaming slab. The men were breathing hard, but there was no need for oxygen.

With his binoculars Bradford scanned the mountain, searching for tracks or a sign of the Snowman. If his idea held up, the monster would not appear until it began to snow. He decided not to tell the men about his theory, simply to order them to be more vigilant when the visibility decreased. Abuting the icefall, he located a sangar, a low rock wall and a natural wind-break. They were on flat ground now, and they walked abreast toward the sangar.

"How was the weight, Jamie?" he asked.

"I can probably handle sixty maximum," the broad-shouldered Indian replied. "I came up with no trouble carrying eighty-five. These oxygen cylinders are ball-breakers."

"You were going pretty fast," Spider complained.

"Yeah," Packard agreed, puffing. "You were going flat out. What happens when we get up real high?"

"Show him, Pemba."

The little Sherpa darted out on the ice, still carrying his full load, and looked like an Olympic sprinter.

"Man, remember me? You didn't hire O.J. but a shitbusted crap shooter fresh out of the slam," Spider informed him. When Pemba returned to the group, Spider asked, "What the hell did they feed you up there in Nepal?"

"Monkeys."

"God help us," Packard said, setting down his pack.

By noon they had set up their three bright orange Meade tents and Bradford had established radio contact with Monte's office with a specially adapted Pioneer shortwave set. It operated on high-tension batteries and would give six hours' use at thirty below. Each of the men had a high-frequency walkie-talkie with crystal controls on both reception and transmission. The walkie-talkies weighed only two pounds and could be carried under their vests, where body heat would insure that they would remain in working order.

"This is Survey One," Bradford said over the radio.

"Come in. This is Base!" Ashby shouted excitedly. "How's the transmission?"

"You're in stereo. Have you seen anything yet?"

"No, we've made our camp on the western edge below the icefall."

"I've got Chuck standing by with the chopper. Should we come up?"

"I wouldn't bother yet. They're heavy winds, and you'll bounce around too much."

"Can you get any pictures?"

"If you want slabs of ice I'll get one of the boys to start shooting. Survey One over and out."

The camp had become a reality, and in spite of the intense cold the constant movement brought them all out in a sweat. Food supplies were stored in one of the tents and two primus stoves were rigged up. At one o'clock a signal came in: Carlos had arrived and would land by helicopter at the camp. None of the elaborate preparations would make any sense if the weapons didn't work.

Bradford climbed over the ice about a quarter of a mile from camp. He had spied an oblong boulder the size of a twenty-ton trailer, and he thought it would provide a fair test of the weapon's capability. He found a flat stretch and radioed his position to the copter pilot. In a few minutes the chopper was above him, its rotors churning in the heavy crosswind. Severely buffeted in the channel between the mountains, it finally landed a few hundred yards ahead of him.

He sent out a message on the walkie-talkie to the men, asking them to reconnoiter below the icefall. The copter's side windows were fogged; Bradford rapped on the door with his ice ax. The pilot opened the door and with Ashby's help shunted out a large black metal box. They set it down on the ice. Monte climbed out, followed by Carlos wrapped in a fur coat. The pilot returned to the chopper, and Monte said curtly to him, "Be back here in thirty minutes, Chuck."

Bradford detected a look of strain on Carlos's face, and it was confirmed when the munitions expert said, "I'll never undertake another job like this. The time pressure was intolerable."

"Do they work?"

"We ran a single test and it was effective."

"But there were complications?" Bradford said.

"I'm afraid so. What seemed so promising on paper didn't quite work out in practice."

Ashby stood to one side, talking into a tape recorder. "Like what?"

"The quantity," Carlos replied with a gesture of helplessness. "I had sixty men working day and night just so you'd have five arrows per man."

"Shit, there's no margin for error."

"Dan, the plutonium itself still made an explosion when it made contact, even though the radioactive nature of the element operates on an implosion principle."

"This is suicidal," Ashby said.

"Butt out of this, Jim," Bradford said, glaring at him.

"We took the warhead and constructed a miniaturized laser made out of plutonium so that on contact the effect is the same but there is no sound."

Carlos stooped down and unlocked the box. A thin lead sheet covered the weapons.

Pemba arrived leading the others; they watched with interest as Carlos lifted a second layer of styrofoam. The box was divided into five compartments, and there were sounds of approval when the men saw the crossbows. They were constructed of a highly polished aluminum compound. Carlos showed them the flex on the aircraft cable and demonstrated the assembly procedure. He attached the automatic firing mechanism to the center of the shaft, then, with a small screwdriver, adjusted the Zeiss telescopic sight.

"You press this button to activate the zoom lens," he explained. He handed the crossbow to Bradford and supervised the men as they assembled the others. He pulled out five brass-fletched practice arrows and handed them out.

"You can use these to see what adjustments you want to make."

"What about the warhead?" Bradford asked.

"I've brought only one to test."

"What's the range?"

"I got it up to a hundred yards."

"Christ, that's practically on top of the target," Spider said, aligning the practice arrow.

They moved out to the boulder. With a knife, Bradford scraped the ice off a section of it until he hit black rock. The sharp contrast would serve as a target.

Bradford paced off a hundred yards. The men took various positions to fire. Packard was crouched; Spider was upright; Jamie kneeled. They sighted the boulder through the telescopic sights. Bradford held a stopwatch, then gave the order to fire individually.

The four shots reached the target area in one and nine tenths seconds. The arrows were within eight inches of one another, and Bradford was satisfied that there was no question of the crossbow's accuracy, although the men made various adjustments. He kept them practicing for twenty minutes, until the shots were within three inches of one another. Because the wind died down for a time, the velocity increased to just over one second.

Bradford signaled Carlos to bring him the armed arrow. It was in a lead container. Bradford examined the warhead. It was cup-shaped and covered with a transparent material. Inside he saw a miniaturized pendulum and copper-colored hammer. He was conscious of Ashby taking pictures of him and said bitterly,

"Now, we're not fucking around playing games. Get the hell back."

Bradford stood upright, set the arrow on the aircraft cable, then pressed the zoom button on the sight, bringing the boulder inches away from his right eye. He released the automatic trigger and watched the flight of the red-fletched arrow.

The arrow struck the exposed patch of rock and adhered. Virtually instantaneously, the boulder began to disintegrate. Huge shards of stone flew into the air; there was a deep smoking hole where the giant boulder had been.

Ashby shielded his eyes from the flash of light, while the men cheered jubilantly. Monte put his arms around Carlos's shoulders and did an absurd little jig with him. The test had been perfect.

"What about fallout and contamination?" Ashby asked.

"Minimal in these conditions."

Bradford nodded and said, "Pay the man, Monte."

"You're a brave but naive man, Dan. You don't think I would have boarded the plane without my money," Carlos said.

"What if it didn't work?" Bradford asked.

"Mr. Dale could have tried to sue me," he said with a complacent air.

The chopper brought them all back to the lodge. During the short trip, Bradford saw the slopes filled with people skiing with various degrees of proficiency. It had begun to snow, and he had deep misgivings. The skiers might be exposed to an attack in these conditions. But there was easy laughter among his team, and he decided to hold back his concern. This was the first time since he recruited them that they were acting like friends with a common purpose. He'd let them take the rest of the day off. They'd begin the climb tomorrow morning.

Outside the warming hut, mobs of people patiently waited in line for their turn on the lifts. A holiday atmosphere was evident in spite of the heavy snow which struck at them. Many of the men wore face masks; the women were colorfully outfitted in fashionable ski suits. A group of young children below the ski school had built a snowman and were pelting it with snowballs.

Bradford watched through his binoculars and remembered how as a boy he had waited in all kinds of weather for his turn to get on the T-bar. He would ski from eight till four, forgetting to eat lunch. The sensation of actually flying when he was coming down a run was embedded in his consciousness. He had been truly free, a boy on a pair of wooden Head skis a bit too long for him, and he had navigated mountains with the joy of someone making a discovery.

When he was no more than eight he had realized that he would never be able to settle down like his parents and their friends. There was too much to do in a short lifetime for him to stay put; he had a secret desire which he nurtured all through his adolescence. He wanted to fly. Not in a plane or a copter, but to take off from the slopes and float through the air. He believed that one day he would. He would leave the slopes at the end of each day in a state of profound exhilaration. Skiing for him was the ultimate high, capturing the magical properties of the unknown. He spent hours during the summer sitting in the town library, poring over maps of mountains; he knew by heart the height of the hundred highest mountains in the world. Everest always held him fast, and before he went to sleep he would chant the Sherpa word for it: *"Chomolungma!* Goddess Mother of the world."

Now he looked up at the slopes and had a moment of regret.

The practice had gone better than Barry had any right to expect. He had skied out of the shoot on the experts' slope. The slope angled downhill to a sheer forty-five degrees. His speed neared seventy miles an hour, and he made perfect christies. He had forced himself back into a routine, even agreeing to teach a beginners' class as therapy.

Unfortunately, his afternoon was spoiled by a difficult pupil. A practical joker by the name of Willie was constantly interrupting him and cutting up. If the kid got out of line one more time, Barry was determined to leave him behind after they skied this run.

He waited a short distance down the slope and called out to a young woman: "Bend your knees and turn."

She did precisely the opposite—leaning back, failing to flex her knees forward—and flopped on her can. He sidestepped up the slope and helped her get back in her right ski. He adjusted the binding. Above them Willie was shouting at the woman, "Fat horse, you need a sled!"

"Shut up, Willie!" Barry called out angrily. It took a great deal for him to lose his cool, but this monster was the limit. Now that the woman was back on her skis, Barry took her arm and guided her down past a mogul. "Press your ankles against your boots so that you feel them, and keep those knees bent," he counseled. They reached the spot near the cross-country trail and stopped. Barry waved on the class one by one; several of them were making progress, which pleased him.

"Okay, Willie, you're doing fine . . ."

Despite his obnoxiousness, the boy had that fearlessness that comes with ignorance. He made two perfect turns, but then, instead of stopping at the rear of the group, he gathered speed and headed directly for the five people in the class. In their anxiety to get out of his way, they were forced to lurch sideways, and they tripped over their skis. The whole class, including Barry, fell.

"Got you, fatso," Willie cawed at the woman, who had just gained some confidence after Barry had led her down. Willie skied past them without losing his balance and headed for the cross-country trail. His middle finger was raised in a "screw you" gesture.

Barry struggled to his feet and shouted, "That's it! You're finished! Now, goddamn it, stop and wait for me!"

Willie skied through the patch of forest alongside the run. A pine forest dense with trees almost sixty feet high blocked off the afternoon sun. The snow from the branches was whipped off in sudden flurries by wind gusts. Willie looked up and saw the gondola cars passing slowly above him. He bent down and picked up a hardened piece of snow. He was transfixed by the bright crystalline light it threw off. He sniggered with delight, visualizing packing soft snow around it and slamming the ski instructor right in the face with it. He put it in his pocket; he would save it for the right moment.

He skied down a small hill. Something in the distance caught his eye. He'd been right last night. He *had* seen something move, trailing the gondola. Surrounding him were a series of enormous wedge-shaped tracks, leading deeper into the forest. If this was a new species of animal and he discovered it, he'd become world-famous and make a fortune. He'd buy all the condominiums and resell them at a huge profit. The tracks led to a clearing, and he peered through some high evergreen bushes to see where they continued. The trail became bumpy, and he almost lost his balance as he tried to separate the bushes to get a better perspective.

He stopped moving when he heard an odd humming sound coming from somewhere behind him. Through the thicket of trees, a sharp ray of light struck a mound of snow beside him. He shielded his eyes from the intense glare and jumped back when the snow burst into flames. It smoked, then turned black, and he began to scream.

The animal was moving toward him. Lurching back to avoid it, Willie fell. It was making a sound like a bear. Long, gnarled fingers groped toward him; then he saw sharp claws flick from the fingers, like switchblade knives.

He began to cry and plead, but the claws ripped at his parka and he was lifted off the ground. He was carried higher and higher, almost to the tops of the trees. Blood oozed from his mouth. The claws were tearing at his flesh. He looked down and saw that his right leg had been torn off· at the hip. He fell into deep shock.

"Willie, Willie, goddamn you, if you're hiding I'll bust your head!" Barry struggled along the narrow cross-country path. He stopped and picked up a short ski pole. "Willie, are you okay?" The snow became heavier, and Barry dropped his goggles and strained to see where he was going. Behind him the snow hissed as though it was on fire, and the smell became putrid as though flesh was burning. Barry wanted to vomit. As he moved more surely now, where the mouth of the path widened, an explosion of blood and tissue descended from above him, drenching him.

"Oh, God, no," he said weakly when he saw the giant horned gray body towering over him. There was a hideous grinding of teeth which threw off blinding sparks, charring his clothes. He flung himself against a tree to put out the fire on his sleeve. He was suddenly seized by his head; teeth were driving demonically through his flesh.

Bradford sat with Cathy on the porch of the warming hut, drinking a rum toddy. His attention was caught by some kind of trouble on the slopes. A siren from the ski patrol resounded frantically. Moving down the center run was an object traveling with tremendous speed, which the skiers were attempting to dodge. Bradford rushed down the metal-runged steps and held up his binoculars.

"What happened?" Cathy asked.

"Oh, shit, no!" he said, dropping the binoculars. "Don't look," he said, turning her away forcibly, but she had already caught a glimpse of it.

"I—" She began to weep, and held her hand to her mouth.

Coming to rest at the ski school was a headless bloody torso with one leg still attached to it.

A sheet of heavy snow obliterated Bradford's vision as he rushed up to the school. People on the slopes were injured, screaming for help, and rolling down head over heels. On the P.A. system, over the siren, a man's voice kept repeating "Code Three, Code Three . . ."

The wailing of the people gained intensity until it reached a crescendo. Ski instructors jammed onto gondolas and lifts in an effort to rescue the people who had fallen. A low underground noise gained force. Gigantic séracs crumbled below the summit and thundered down the runs in enormous blocks, creating tremendous fissures in the ice.

The mountain itself appeared to cleave open for an instant as the avalanche spread, jarring eaves of snow into enclosed valleys on the mountain's flanks. These cwms overflowed with snow and ice and were unable to contain the rocks and boulders which came down in a steady, unrelenting cascade.

Bradford helped a middle-aged man to his feet, then grabbed hold of two crying children and carried them down to ground level. Ambulances and police sirens whined in the background.

In just over an hour the lodge resembled a military field hospital. Dozens of people had broken arms and legs; others had suffered fractured skulls and concussion.

Nine were dead.

Chapter Sixteen

Cathy watched the gondola taking the men up the mountain. The wind cut at her face as she tried to keep it in sight; she wanted to keep alive the final brief moment she had had with Bradford. When most of the injured had been carried to ambulances, he had assembled his men outside the lodge. Then he had taken her aside and put his arms around her.

"I'll be back."

"I won't count on it," she replied.

"It wouldn't have mattered to me one way or the other a while ago, but now it does."

The gondola vanished and she headed back to the lodge. There was a crush of people in the lobby— grieving and panic-stricken, searching for their mates and lost children. Squads of state troopers tried to restore order, and one of the officers kept repeating over the loudspeaker: "Keep calm. Please return to your rooms. Don't attempt to leave yet. The roads have to be kept free for rescue squads." His voice was drowned out by caterwauling cries of terror and hysteria. People were being knocked down as others flooded the exits. There was no place that was safe.

Cathy slipped out of an emergency exit in the bar and ran toward Monte's office. Red and amber lights on the mass of squad cars wormed a dizzying pattern as they flashed across her line of sight. She became disoriented for a few moments and leaned against the porch rail of a deserted town house. The door was open; skis, boots, and clothing were scattered on the floor. Water was running in a bathtub which had overflowed; it seeped slowly across the floor. She caught her breath and pushed through a group of reporters, who had arrived in helicopters from all over the state. Cameramen with miniaturized hand-held cameras panned across the shattered runs. Interviewers shoved microphones in the shocked faces of eyewitnesses, who babbled incoherently about the avalanche.

She knocked on Monte's locked door and shouted her name. The door opened a few inches, and Ashby let her in. The phones rang, but no one in the room seemed to have the will to answer them. She took the receivers off and looked from Ashby to the sheriff. Monte sat numbly at his desk, impotent and frightened.

"What are we going to say?" she insisted.

"Ice weakness caused by an earthquake," Ashby said.

"Jim, you've all been lying to me. Now I want to hear the truth. No one's going to believe that we had a tremblor. Something killed those people on the mountain," the sheriff insisted. "The same thing that attacked that girl?"

"There's a giant bear loose . . . a new strain that nobody knew existed," Monte said.

"You've sent a group of men up there. Are they game hunters?" Garson asked.

"Yes," Ashby said. "Monte brought them in when he realized that there wasn't anyone local who could handle it."

"Jim, why didn't you tell me this at the beginning? Your friendship isn't worth a damn," Garson said. He looked scornfully at the three of them. "I had a responsibility. I'm going to have to swing for this—and so help me, I'll put the three of you under arrest for withholding evidence if I don't get the truth."

People were pounding on the door, and Garson picked up his walkie-talkie and instructed his men to clear the building and ask the state trooper captain to come up.

Inside the gondola Bradford scanned the mountain with his binoculars. Contour lines had altered; he could make out through the sheets of snow new fissures in the glacier—crevasses of great depth running in crazy zigzag patterns. The scope of the avalanche had not been as great as it had first seemed from ground level.

He was worried about the condition of base camp; if it was buried they would have to return to the lodge and wait for more equipment to arrive from L.A. But as they moved higher the weather was clearer. The storm had changed direction, which was in their favor.

They left the gondola at the experts' slope and broke into three parties, Bradford's consisting of himself alone. They were at the source of the avalanche and could not begin to climb higher until they tested the stability of the lower slopes. They would be forced to use dynamite at this altitude and hope that the upper slopes would not be disturbed.

Bradford gave out hand charges of dynamite for them to set off at various points of the mountain, in an effort to shift the weak walls of snow and ice and allow the huge mass of rock to consolidate. He could see that the various depressions were now blocked with ice; this would make the climb easier.

He gave the others the simpler tasks of skiing to the intermediate and beginners' slopes. He would blast at the higher runs. He nervously skied under a new cornice, the mass of snow precariously overhanging a contorted ridge. He set off two charges on four minute fuses, dropped them under the cornice, and skied along rock stubble into a wooded copse which the avalanche had bypassed. He jammed cotton into his ears. The blast shook the ground beside him and shifted a group of screes filled with loose stones under the cornice.

At a signal, Packard and Spider skied down to the intermediate slopes and repeated the action beside a moraine where debris had been brought down from the snout of the glacier. Jamie and Pemba were at about thirty-five hundred feet on the lower slopes, and they skied in opposite directions to clear two immense sèracs which had blocked the runs. In twenty minutes the three groups had set off forty charges, and it was with a sense of relief that Bradford studied the mountain for any further sign of weakness. He discovered that it had firmed up; it would become more durable as the temperature dropped.

They reconnoitered at the gondola hut when he sounded a hand siren. The climb up to the base in the waning sunlight was not as difficult as he had anticipated. They were on familiar terrain, and the route was girdled to avoid newly formed screes. The sangar had been out of the path of the avalanche and the camp remained as it had been left. Bradford checked the radio transmission.

"This is Survey One," Bradford said over the mike.

"Identify yourself," Sheriff Garson answered.

"Who is this?"

"Sheriff Garson. Repeat, identify yourself."

"Daniel Bradford."

"How many men are with you?"

"Four."

"Okay, Bradford. Get your men together and come down."

"I can't. We dynamited, and the area around the lifts is blocked."

"Well, then give me your grid position and we'll send a rescue helicopter up for you."

"The weather's bad," Bradford lied.

"Can you hang in till morning?"

"Sheriff, we're not coming down."

"Look, if you don't you'll all be under arrest. The mountain's been officially closed by my office." When there was no response, he asked, "Do you read me?"

Bradford had closed down the radio transmission, but Garson persisted. "Bradford, I don't want you dead. Now fire some flares . . ."

Garson shook his head disconsolately and said to Ashby, "You disgust me . . . anything for a story."

Ashby sensed that he had Garson boxed in. He could still manipulate him so that he would come away with his trophy.

"Pat, I'm not going to apologize, but I'm going to give you some realistic advice. If you go out there and tell those vultures that you believe there's a Snowman on the mountain, you'll be finished. There's no real evidence yet. Sure, you can show them the pictures of the footprints, but who's to say they weren't doctored? And you can't show the pictures of the girl or they'll hang you for keeping quiet so long. Stick with the story of a giant bear and an ice weakness and you've got a chance to ride through this. Especially since you've got professional climbers already up there.

"I'll run a special edition describing how you took control of the situation. The choice is yours. Either you come out a hero or an incompetent who didn't know what the hell was going on in his own town. You'll be vulnerable, and no matter what you say to the contrary, it'll look like you were part of a conspiracy to hush this up because you wanted to protect vested interests. Man, they'll send a couple of hot-shit reporters down from L.A. and they'll eat you alive because I'll co-operate with them. So before you shoot your mouth off, think about it . . . you'll be spending the rest of your life in courtrooms and giving lawyers depositions. I wouldn't want to see you in that position."

Garson shambled out of the room, broken and dispirited.

In the kitchen tent, Pemba cut thick slices from the smoked pork they had brought up. He fried them with eggs and pinto beans on the primus stove and boiled some snow to make coffee, which he spiked with rum.

After dinner, Spider took charge. He brought out cards and started a four-handed game of low-ball, which took the men's minds off what lay ahead.

The first day's climb would be the hardest, because they would have to establish a temporary camp on the icefall. They'd all be carrying upwards of forty pounds of weight, and both Spider and Packard would have trouble breathing without oxygen in the rarefied air. The going would be slow and laborious.

Crouched low outside his tent to avoid the violent hack of the night wind, Bradford stared into the darkness. The sky was bright with clusters of stars; he prayed for snow during the day rather than at night, so that when the Snowman came out they'd have a better chance at him. He decided to initiate a three-hour watch, which would give them all six hours of sleep. He had brought along a supply of Doriden as well as Dexedrine to combat drowsiness. The lack of humidity would cause them all to have insomnia for several nights until they adjusted to the sharp, arid, dehydrating air. The pills would allow them to have uninterrupted sleep until they were acclimatized.

He shone his flashlight up the flank of the slope. Perhaps the Snowman responded to light. Was there any way to bring him out, or were they completely at his mercy?

He took out his ice ax and climbed a short distance above the camp, so that he could get some perspective on the Snowman's path of attack if he left his hiding place during the night. Would it merely be snow that brought him out, or some other primitive instinct? Could he smell or see them now? Was he watching? Did he attack only for food or to defend his new domain? If only there was some way to incite an attack so that they could be ready for him.

Bradford was on a small, firm, rectangular snow-packed shelf, exposed to the wind; sharp-honed ice needles bit into his skin. He listened to the men complain when Pemba won a pot. They'd be all right; Pemba would hold them together. Bradford flashed the light at another section, and in the whine of the wind he thought he heard the muffled cry of an animal.

He climbed down from the shelf and headed for his tent. He set his wrist alarm for midnight, the curfew he had imposed on the men. He would take the first watch. He pulled off his boots and climbed into the rectangular sleeping bag. The bulky ensolite pad was raw with cold, and made his skin burn on contact. He rolled over on his side and softly chanted, *"Om Mane Padme Om . . ."* until his lids became heavy and he saw Cathy's face touching his.

The gray morning carried gelid blasts of air which bit into their faces. Pemba wore a Sherpa balaclava. The woolen hood covered his head and neck and left only a small opening for his face, which was coated with oil.

Ahead of him, on the ice wall, Spider turned, shivering, and demanded in outrage, "What the hell's that stink you giving off? I never smelled that brand of suntan oil."

"It's goose fat," Pemba said, laughing.

"Goose fat! Lay some of it on me, monkey. My skin feels like a bear's ass."

Nearing a great outcropping of rock, Bradford paused and fired his spring-loaded harpoon. A grapnel landed in the spur, and Bradford cut the trail ahead. He pulled hard at the rope to insure that the grapnel was anchored. He then passed the rope from man to man so that they could climb belayed. When he reached the top of the spur he found himself on a platform leading to the icefall. The step was a gigantic frozen cascade of ice. The surface of the glacier was badly split from the avalanche. Tottering blocks of ice hung on feathery threads of snow. The glacier itself was in a constant state of change and movement. He heard ominous underground noises as the gut of the glacier expanded and contracted.

The team scoured the flanks of the mountain from the platform. The fresh snow overlying the existing layer made the direct route too dangerous; it was unstable and could peel off in avalanches. Heavy eaves of snow near the summit leaned forward portentously. Ahead of them crevasses appeared, widening and closing with startling suddenness. In the distance Bradford made out a shape of some kind, but even with his binoculars he could not identify it. He and Pemba decided to go ahead, leaving the others to rest.

As their crampons crunched into the ice, Bradford spied a series of barely discernible tracks crisscrossing a pitch. It seemed impossible for anything to have climbed that stretch of icy rock between the ledges above the icefall.

"Yeti," Pemba said nervously.

"Could be." He tried to control his nervousness.

They were above fifteen thousand feet, traversing the icefall, and as they moved in a northerly direction, the snowfall increased, slowing them down. If any place was ideal for an encounter with the Snowman, this was it. On this flat surface there was no danger of falling. The team could spread out and encircle the Snowman in a pincers attack, cutting off any retreat.

They lowered their snow goggles and made for the object that Bradford had seen. It was difficult to judge distances over the vast icefall. They were shocked by how fast they reached it, and more so when they saw what it was. Lying exposed on the icefall was the severed body of Barry Harkness. The eyes had been gouged out, and the sockets were filled with slivers of ice. Part of the trunk had been eaten, and there were deep zigzagging wounds as though he had been thrust into an industrial saw. His hair had turned white, and sections of his skull had been torn open. Bradford stooped down and with his ice ax began to dig up blocks of hardened snow. In a moment, Pemba was helping him in the grizzly job of burial.

"He was carried up here and left," Bradford said.

Pemba shook his head ruefully. He laid his red Khada scarf on the mound of ice.

"I don't want you to tell the others."

"Kai chai na."

"But it does matter," Bradford insisted. "They'll run out on us."

They staggered back across the desolate frozen plain of ice and snow. Sharp waves of ice granules bit into their skin. It was like hacking their way through a frozen white jungle.

The five men decided to establish a provision dump at the base of the icefall. Later that afternoon, when the weather cleared, they located a negotiable pass running beside the icefall so that they could girdle the peaks beyond their position. They made a diagonal traverse across the top of the spur, reaching an altitude of sixteen thousand eight hundred feet.

Bradford was following the tracks he had seen earlier. They were covered with fresh snow. He cautioned the men to be ready to use their crossbows at any moment.

Chapter Seventeen

All the guests had now been evacuated from the lodge, and as Cathy peered out of the window at the disaster area she spied only highway patrolmen erecting barriers and newsmen huddled in small groups passing thermoses of coffee. Garson had been forced into a bind and was now under control. He had stuck to Ashby's account of the tragedy, but he had been pressured to reveal that a party of big-game hunters were now tracking the bear. He refused to give further details, and closed the mountain to any but official air traffic.

Monte had spent most of the day on the telephone talking to Wright and trying to explain what had occurred. His face was drained of all color, and he could hardly string two coherent sentences together.

The state of confusion in his office was maddening. Salesmen were lined up demanding their checks; the captain of the highway patrol was on the phone to the National Guard, who were waiting for approval from the governor's office. A new batch of journalists were on their way from the national magazines.

"I suggested to the National Guard that we bomb the mountain," the highway patrol captain said confidently. "That way, whatever the hell's up there won't get another chance."

"What're you talking about?" Cathy protested. "Five men are up there. You can't bomb them."

"Hell no, just get them on the shortwave and order them down."

Sheriff Garson pointed to the set.

"Care to try raising them, Captain? I'd be obliged if you could. We've been trying to make contact all day, but there's a storm up there and just a little interference."

"You've lost contact with them?" he asked in astonishment.

"Afraid so," Ashby replied. "Now, have you got any idea what might happen to the town, not to mention the rest of the state, if you try to bomb?" He pointed at the colored relief map on the wall. "Here's Convict Lake and here's the Jeffrey Pine Forest, which leads up to Minaret Summit. This area is filled with volcanic domes. And as you can see, there's an earthquake fault right in the middle. This is only one of hundreds of fractures in the glassy volcanic rock covering the mountain. So bomb away, and we'll just head down to Berkeley and keep an eye on the seismograph. If you get lucky we might get a biggie on the Richter scale—maybe a nine-five. And that, Captain Olafson, ought to get you a nice place in the history books."

Olafson looked despondently at several of his men, who were standing by the fireplace warming themselves.

"Then what the hell do we do?"

"We've got five experts on the mountain, led by Daniel Bradford. They've got weapons, they know what to expect," Monte said with assurance. "I hired them for this job."

At the door a mob of journalists had gathered and were shouting angrily for an interview with Monte Dale. Cathy went into the corridor to fend them off. Bright lights were switched on, and she was blinded by the unexpected glare. She was bombarded by questions, and she decided not to answer any of them until she was allowed to read a statement she had prepared earlier.

"If I can have your attention for a moment, I'd like to try to explain what happened today."

The room quieted down. The TV mini cameras rolled, and she cleared her voice.

"In all the survey work that was done before Great Northern Development decided to build a ski village and develop ski runs here, there was no indication that there was a geological weakness in Sierra Mountain. We may never know exactly what caused the avalanche, but right now we're trying to find out with a team of five surveyors up the mountain, headed by an expert climber named Daniel Bradford."

A voice from the back of the room boomed out, "Our research department ran a check on Bradford. He went after a Snowman years ago. Now why would he be the one you'd bring in if you thought a bear and an avalanche had killed those people?"

Cathy ignored the question and returned to the office.

* * *

179

The team had covered half of the icefall by late afternoon. Surrounding them were frost-riven spires. Packard was having difficulty breathing even with the oxygen, and he was slowing them down. Just ahead of them was a cwm, a small enclosed valley on the flank of the spur; it would be a good site for a supply dump.

The men were exhausted, staggering like drunks. Bradford knew he was pushing them too hard, but he needed to use the last hours of light in order to block off the principal route the Snowman could use.

The tracks he had been following were now covered by snow, but he could trace their path by the deep declivities that appeared at irregular intervals. He was able to work out a rough formula of how large the Snowman's strides were by pacing off the indentations. The figure he arrived at was approximately eight feet, which indicated that the Snowman must be at least twenty-five feet tall. When he had seen him at Lhotse it had been impossible in his panic to get any exact idea of his size.

The radio transmission was set up by Spider and Packard, but the signals were blocked by the mountain chain. Rather than waste batteries, they closed down.

Jamie took over the kitchen chores and boiled some snow for soup. They set up a small tent and unloaded the supplies they had brought up.

"What do you think?" Bradford asked Pemba.

"Let's go on ahead and see where the tracks lead."

"Did the others notice them?"

"I doubt it."

"What are we going to do with Packard?" Bradford asked.

"He can't handle the altitude, but he's the best shot."

"I'll leave him in charge of the supply dump to protect our rear."

Above them was the great saddle of the Sierra Col, a depression on the face buttressing the summit. It was obscured by iron-colored clouds and continuous sheets of snow. The men slithered across the ice, stopping every few feet, hunched over in the wind. A low, vibrating sound, different from the ice movement, was coming from a source near the summit. It was rhythmical and had no timbre.

"Christ!" Bradford began taking shelter against an arête. "It sounds like a heart."

They stood transfixed in the narrow rock passage, intimidated and thrilled by the possibility that they had located the Snowman. In a crevasse to the side, swollen like a large gray vein, were the remains of a Kodiak. It had been flattened against the ice wall; they would have to cross the corpse to reach the summit.

Bradford noticed an odd saline odor that was reminiscent of the sea at low tide. If only he'll stay put, he thought.

By the time he and Pemba returned to camp, Bradford had worked out a plan which would enable them to mousetrap the Snowman. It depended on Packard's remaining as a backup.

He drew a triangle on the map and said, "We'll form two groups—Spider and I, Pemba and Jamie. We'll use a rope ladder to cross the crevasse below the summit, then the two groups can move toward the summit. All we want to do is rouse him. Then we'll form a wedge and strike in a pincer move and hope he'll respond to the sound or the smell. We hit him once he comes down this pinnacle of ice."

"You're assuming he'll act predictably," Packard

said. "Man, we made assumptions like that about the V.C. in Nam, and believe me, our plans weren't worth two shits."

"He's lodged behind the sérac," Pemba said. "There's no other way down this side of the mountain."

"There may be for him. We have to climb whatever's negotiable—he doesn't. But what we're counting on is his instinct to attack," Bradford explained.

"How can you be sure that he's not below us?" Spider asked edgily. "Could be he's cut us off."

"I heard him, and so did Pemba."

The men avoided looking at Bradford. The fire glowed in the center of the tent. The walls were frozen from the condensation of their breath. Outside the winds swept to gale force, bellowing between the sérac and the mountainside.

"It's time for a weapon-assembly drill," Bradford ordered.

Working with their gloves on, they fitted the riser with two aluminum limbs, then flexed the limbs on two pulleys rotated on the wire aircraft cable. They mounted their sniper scopes and took the firing position. Bradford kept them at the drill for an hour and managed to get their routine down to two minutes and forty seconds. Outside on the mountain even with ideal weather conditions, they'd be fortunate to break four minutes.

"We'll have to climb with them assembled," he said at the end. It was bad luck, since they ran the danger of having the bow freeze. The aluminum might begin to contract at certain sub-zero temperatures.

"Suits me," Spider said. "I never liked the idea of putting my piece together when I'm ready to fire it."

Relieved that he no longer was required to climb,

Packard volunteered to take the first watch. Spider followed him outside when the others were asleep. They huddled against the ice wall to keep out of the direction of the wind.

"I don't like leaving you behind," Spider said.

"Shit, I can't hack the climb is all. At close range the bows'll work. But I think you're going to have to get a lot closer than a hundred yards. This wind'll blow a bullet off course." Packard opened his parka and revealed a .357 Magnum. "I'm not taking any chances, which is why I brought junior along with three boxes of ammo."

"I've got some plastique in my kick. If it comes to it, avalanche or not, I've got enough to blow that mother to Saigon. You didn't expect an old pro like me to go fighting with bows and arrows. Shit, if we're going to war, the Spider-Man's bringing his own deck."

There was a hollow uncertainty in their soft conspiratorial laughter. Shards of ice lashed viciously at Spider as he struggled back to the tent. The starless night frightened him. More than ever he wished he had remained safe in the East Vegas jail. Perched on an elbow in his sleeping bag, he looked up at the tent roof and muttered to himself, "Hard way four . . . twenty-two come up smiling."

183

Chapter Eighteen

By the time they reached the crevasse in the morning, it was covered. A snow bridge had formed across it. Bradford attached himself to Pemba's snap-link to test its stability. He walked stealthily, like a nervous burglar. As he crossed it, ice channels shifted between huge troughs.

"We'll use the rope ladder," he called out. At the sound of his voice, the moat shuddered, dropping a wall of snow down a gulley of inestimable depth. It was as though a wound ran through the body of ice. Surface tremors appeared, revealing further ice weaknesses. The glare from the sun on the glacier was blinding.

Pemba fired a grapnel, and Bradford hammered it into a shelf with his ice ax. He tied the heavy nylon ladder to another section, jamming it into the open head of a steel piton. The rope bridge extended for ten feet.

Spider cringed when he was waved onto it. His face was raw from the cold, and he inched his way along the ladder, moving on his belly. When he reached the other side, he collapsed. Jamie was next; he shied away like a frightened horse. Bradford bullied him into crossing. Midway over, the ice below him splintered; he lay frozen with terror on the rope.

"Don't look down," Pemba pleaded. "You're almost there."

Bradford held out his hand to encourage him.

"I can't—"

"Jamie, you've got to move," Bradford insisted as the splinters widened into throbbing veins.

Crippled with fear, Jamie lay prone, gasping in the rarefied air. Another block of ice fell below him, creating a hissing cataract in the crevasse. Finally, Jamie forced himself to grope his way over to the other side, where he fell to his knees as though stricken.

Pemba was the last to come, wiggling adroitly and seemingly without fear. Now they were all on the other side of the slowly disintegrating moat. Pemba and Bradford pulled the ladder with them. As they stepped away, the gap widened, ice crackling, until the crevasse shattered. It was now almost the length of a city block. They watched in helpless frustration as they found themselves cut off from their camp and Packard.

They were on a cleaver, an island of granite rock sheathed with ice, circling the body of the glacier. Above them the dazzling bare-faced walls of the summit rose like threatening daggers.

"We'll never get down again!" Spider shouted.

"Don't be crazy," Bradford said. "We'll make it."

When he found his voice, Jamie joined the protest. "Dan, we were going to wait for the Snowman to come and get us. Why're we tracking him?"

"Because we couldn't wait and find ourselves trapped."

"He's luring us up the mountain," Spider said. "Man, you fell for the bait."

It was a dead-end argument—useless to continue. Bradford took out his walkie-talkie, raised the aerial, and spoke into it.

"This is Bradford—come in, Camp Two."

In a moment Packard's voice crackled over the line.

"Camp Two. How are you mothers?"

"We're okay. We'll have to come down to you a different way. We're at the southeast corner of the ice-fall. Grid numbers forty-seven sixty-one. Try to get through to the ground when the weather clears and give them our position."

"Roger. Hey, listen, anything happening?"

"Not yet. How's it down below?"

"Beautiful. I've got my swimsuit on, and I'm going to take a walk to see if I can pick up a chick with big jugs I spotted on the beach."

"Over and out."

Bradford led the men to a bergschrund. The large crevasse was securely fixed on the upper slope of a glacier separating it from the steeper slopes of ice above them. They were a good eight hundred feet below the summit.

Bradford decided to wait until he detected some movement from the Snowman. The weather was fair now, the snowstorms of only short duration. The Snowman would not come out until the conditions became severe.

Time passed all too slowly for Packard. He failed to reach the sheriff. The signal was weak; he recharged the batteries but still could not make contact. He cleaned up the tent, made himself a can of pork and beans for lunch, dipped saltine crackers into it, and pretended he was eating a real Texas chili. He located Bradford's grid marks on the map, then found himself growing sleepy. He had planned to get some air, but the snowstorm had intensified at his level on the mountain.

He started daydreaming about returning to his ranch, the commotion he would cause at the bank when he deposited his fifty thousand dollars. Curled up in his sleeping bag, he had a smile on his face as he fell into a deep sleep.

It was a while before he reacted to the scraping noises he heard outside the tent. He wondered if they were natural to the mountain. He'd become accustomed to the noise the ice made when the wind lifted it and hurled it against the frozen rock.

But this was different. It was like someone grinding glass on concrete. He put on his boots and his parka, tied the hood, and peered out suspiciously. He couldn't see much. The snowfall was building high drifts on the level shelf of the camp. On impulse he picked up his bow. He was sorry now that he had agreed to stay behind. He could have managed the climb if he used his oxygen. They should have drawn lots, he told himself.

He wasn't sure if the wind was playing tricks. It was impossible, but he thought he heard the mewing of a cat, ululant and insistent. How could an animal survive outside? Yet the sound gained resonance. His uneasiness grew. If only he could see it. He was trying to reach Bradford on the shortwave when he was interrupted by an unexpected movement against the tent. The walls were swaying, and he jumped back, crashing into the stove and upsetting the pot of coffee on it.

"What is it?" he shouted.

The wall of the tent was torn open; something with huge claws slashed at his stores. Cans burst open. He backed away, not knowing what to do. He threw down the crossbow and pulled out his Magnum. He began to fire, round after round, at the claws which groped out blindly. His radio was smashed; the tent collapsed.

Packard struggled to get outside and reloaded. Where was it? He saw a shadowy outline of something enormous. He opened his parka, located the plastic cord, and flung it at the shadow. The explosion threw off blocks of ice and stone. But whatever was out there had not stopped. Now it was thrashing the air in a frenzy.

He staggered back. Something took hold of him, and he shrieked. It began squeezing him; he felt his hand go limp; the pain was intolerable.

"God, God, please help me," he whined. He was lifted high into the air. The wind battered him; he flailed desperately. Something hot and as foul as an infection made him sick; he began to vomit uncontrollably. Then, for the first time since he was an infant, he felt himself void involuntarily.

He struggled away from the rows of spikelike teeth which gnashed so hard that sparks flew, illuminating the head of the Snowman.

He stared at the gleaming eyes; then he was inside those jaws. The teeth locked around his ribs. As he lost consciousness, he heard himself cry; then he began to choke in his own blood.

He was being eaten.

There was no sign of life as, belayed, they climbed up the mountain. They were on a stretch of difficult ice between ledges. The flanks of the pitch were almost vertical, part rock, part ice, seamed with snow-filled gullies which spilled onto the lower slopes. The mountain widened, and they found themselves on a small plateau.

Bradford was hunched over, gasping for breath. Exposed to the biting cold, the men giddily stumbled around. They would have to rest.

The storm was changing direction, traveling north; below him Bradford saw a raging ocean of snow. Above the plateau the sky had turned a hard Prussian blue. For the first time in hours the visibility had improved.

"Put on your oxygen masks," he said in a hoarse voice, choking on the words. The air was so dry that he could not swallow. He adjusted the oxygen nozzle and his lungs heaved. The oxygen was intoxicating; he felt his heart leap. When he had gained control of himself after a few moments, he walked out ahead of the group, examining the plateau with his binoculars. Beyond them were patches of fresh blood, forming a trail. Pemba moved cautiously alongside him.

"Tracks."

"He's left the summit."

They walked ahead, leaving Jamie and Spider. As they approached the trail of blood, Pemba pointed to something on the ice. They halted uncertainly. Pemba stooped and with his ax touched the ice-crusted lump of raw, purplish flesh.

"It's a Kodiak's paw," he said. "A cub."

They followed the path of blood. They were now some distance from the other two men, who wearily tried to catch up. Ahead were gnarled cornices, overhanging masses of snow and ice which jutted out menacingly. It was difficult to hear in the gale winds which scoured the furrows of the summit, but still the unmistakable pitch of a roar carried down to them. They stopped and stood back to back, scanning the mountainside, until they could locate the source. They heard it again, a perverse growl distorted by large ice chimneys which acted as echo chambers.

"Let's go back, Dan."

"Not yet."

In the distance Spider's and Jamie's orange suits appeared as mere specks in the jungle of snow. They were, however, growing larger, closing in on them. Bradford held up his glasses and watched them running. Slithering behind them on all fours was a monstrously large Kodiak. Bradford rushed toward them. The Kodiak was closing the distance.

"Don't fall, goddamn it, don't fall!" he shouted.

He lifted the crossbow off his right shoulder and peeled off his top layer of gloves so he could move his hands. The silk gloves he wore underneath were warm with sweat; he was able to flex his fingers. He took out an armed arrow and fitted it into the cable, then lined up the bear in the telescopic sight. He pressed the zoom button bringing the bear into close-up. The gradations on the lens indicated that the bear was a hundred and fifty yards away.

"The fucker's out of range," he cried. "Keep coming, baby."

Saliva and mucus dripped from the Kodiak's mouth as its face loomed larger in the sight. The bestial rage was horrifying, and it lashed out with its claws at Jamie's back as he slowed up, winded by the pursuit. Bradford moved in. The bear was closing . . .

"One fifteen, one-oh-five," he said, aiming at the deep barrel chest.

He released the automatic trigger, and there was a whip sound which jarred him. Suddenly the Kodiak stopped, numbed by the shock, and the men turned as the air was filled with great masses of bleeding flesh. Bradford watched with amazement.

"It's disintegrating!" he shouted to Pemba.

"I see."

"Shit, it really works!"

The ice was filled with a misshapen bloody patch; nothing remained of the Kodiak. Bradford approached the men, who had fallen face down. The blood was being absorbed by the fresh snow, and only an outline was evident. No tissue, skin, or fur was left. Spider struggled to his knees and pressed his hands together in a gesture of supplication.

"Man, I wanna go home."

"Never saw anything like it," Jamie said. "We should have had these when we were fighting the U.S. Cavalry."

"Then the niggers and the Indians would have inherited the earth," Spider said, rejoicing. "Shit, Dan, that Snowman was enormous!" he added.

Pemba had a quizzical expression. "Snowman?"

"What then?"

"A Kodiak bear."

"No, don't tell me we've got more on our asses."

"It was a female whose cub was killed by the Snowman."

"How do you know that?" Jamie asked with alarm.

"We found part of another bear up ahead."

They spent the next hour attempting to contact

Packard. The channel was clear, but he did not respond.

The crevasse they had crossed earlier continued to widen. The Snowman inched along the platform for almost a quarter of a mile, until he found a gap that was narrow enough for him to straddle. He listened to the movement of the men on the plateau and strode up the side of the bergschrund, following the guy ropes they had left.

The snowstorm had begun again, and he blended in perfectly with the ice and rock. At a depression in the mountainside he stopped; he had heard some vibrations which indicated an ice weakness in a wave of snow nearby. When the sounds weakened, he thrashed at a cornice which was in danger of falling. He dislodged it and found an opening which would lead him to the plateau. He was now directly beneath the men. His claws bored into the side of the mountain, as he burrowed through the ice, forming a deep, undulating channel.

Chapter Nineteen

Darkness came unexpectedly. Bradford led his struggling band under the arch of a solid sérac. They huddled together and ate dry rations. The moment of triumph they had shared at the success of the weapon was forgotten. Bradford was troubled by Spider's silence. He and Jamie seemed to have lost their spirit; he knew how dangerous that was, for without it, the instinct for survival would go. He had seen men in this state before; invariably they were lost. But he was determined not to allow the Snowman to claim any more sacrifices.

It was impossible to sleep, but he decided to withhold sleeping pills. An attack might come at any time.

Pemba whispered to him, "Something's moving."

"Where?"

He pointed to a dull glow emanating from under the ice. It was a diffuse beam that covered a small area.

"Under the ice."

"It could be the radiation from the warhead."

Pemba shook his head doubtfully. "I think we ought to go on ahead."

"If we leave them, they'll panic."

"Dan, I don't think we've got any choice."

Bradford located his flashlight in his pack and checked the batteries. All that remained was a half-life. He stalked out on the ice with Pemba without explaining to the others what he was doing, but neither Spider nor Jamie had the energy to follow; they just stared, haunted and cowed.

The light had spread over a wide area by the time Bradford and Pemba reached a pitch running alongside the ridge. The ice was illuminated, sparkling like glass, when the light struck a prism, rainbows appeared, which added to the eeriness of this possessed mountain.

"He's penetrated the glacier," Bradford said fearfully. "He's been tracking us," he added. "It must be a combination of sound waves and smell that rouses him."

Odd animalistic sounds echoed beneath their feet, but there was no sign of the Snowman. It almost seemed as if, having entrapped them, the monster was now toying with them.

It would be suicidal to fire an arrow into the glacier to draw him out. The mountain would fracture; there would be no way to escape an ice avalanche. They continued along the perimeter of the ridge in an attempt to find the source of the light. As they trod the precipitous path, Bradford could not overcome the conviction that a snare was being laid for them. The light flashed on and off as though some form of primeval code was being used, almost as if the Snowman was attempting to communicate with them. When they left the shelter of the spur, the wind churned, flinging darts of ice in their faces. The pursuit was hopeless; they turned back.

It was an interminable night. Bradford's eyes were raw, and he had difficulty adjusting to the corruscating reflections of sunlight at daybreak. Ice caps mirrored the light; as they climbed the vertical face leading to the summit, they had to pause every few feet because they were blinded.

The terrain was intractable, the progress frustratingly slow. At every bitter, bone-crunching step, the mountain presented new obstacles. Bradford drove his ax into the ice and hacked his way to the upper rim. At the summit he would have an overview of the mountain, be able to detect any movement by the Snowman. At least, that was his hope. But somehow the Snowman had cut them off from Packard. Bradford could not establish radio contact with him. He was worried. A lone man on a mountain had only to slip and twist his ankle outside his tent and he would freeze to death in a matter of minutes.

Heavy, leaden clouds like vultures massing for a carcass hung over the summit. The men stopped below it to adjust their oxygen canisters. Bradford surveyed the assault route to the top. He removed some étriers from his backpack. They would have to use these short rope ladders, anchored by a steel spike, to climb the sharply angled face.

As he and Pemba drove in the spikes and joined ladders, his attention was caught by the wind blowing down a mound of loose stones from a scree. The mountain under him rumbled, and then the air was permeated by a series of violent roars.

"Jamie!" he shouted helplessly as the young Indian

reacted sluggishly, dazed by the sudden crash of an ice wall. Bradford saw him struggling.

Moving from behind him was a huge male Kodiak. Jamie's exposure as the last man was precarious. The vertical drop beneath him was over five thousand feet. He grasped hold of the étriers, but the bear plucked him off the ladder and viciously flung him onto the ice. Jamie's shrieks were muffled by the enraged bear, which savaged him with his claws. The Kodiak lifted Jamie off the ground and tore at his face and throat. Jamie was stripped of his oxygen mask. Blood spurted from a wound in his throat. Pemba and Bradford were immobilized on the ladder and could not free themselves to fire their crossbows.

"Spider! Spider, help him!" Pemba cried out in desperation as he clung to the ladder.

They lost Jamie for a moment, and when they struggled down, Spider was crouched over with the crossbow in his hand. They leaned over the precipice and saw that Jamie was too far below them, splayed across the ice.

"My hands are frozen," Spider said, boggle-eyed.

Bradford took the bow, and as he set himself to fire the mountain seemed to burst open, blocking his view. Thrusting upward through the thick ice platform was the hand of the Snowman. The arm became visible, and the Kodiak lunged at it. Its teeth dug into the Snowman's hand and broke into splinters. In an instant the Snowman shattered the ice, which flew in a shower of hail. He towered over the Kodiak, and as the two beasts struggled, Jamie slipped off the ice. His body floated crazily thousands of feet down an infinite abyss. The Snowman's hands tore through the belly of the Kodiak and a torrent of blood gushed on the ice. The Kodiak groaned and was lifted off its feet and brought to the mouth of the Snowman. The cavernous mouth opened, and in a single echoing crunch the bear was decapitated. The still-writhing trunk was flung against an arête below.

The Snowman was climbing into range. His gray body was blood-spattered, and his maddened eyes were directed at the men.

"I've got him in the sight!" Bradford cried. In a moment he released the trigger, and the arrow adhered to the Snowman's arm. The air was suddenly filled with a foul-smelling black siltlike mucus. The arm began to dissolve. The mountain came alive with a frenzy of sound—one moment a mountain lion, then the roar of a bear as the Snowman lurched from one side to the other. Bradford and Pemba were poised for the next shot, but the Snowman had crawled beneath a sérac, using it as a shield. The ice was blackened by the outline of tissue and ganglia.

"You got the bastard," Spider said softly. Then his triumph gave way to hysteria, and he keened, "Jamie. Jamie. Oh, my God!"

They could not stay on the platform, which took the brunt of a shrill crosswind. Bradford's mind was slowing; he recognized the danger signals. He was beginning to freeze. They had to get to a sheltered area. He placed Spider in the middle, and they climbed lethargically up the rungs of the étriers until they came to a sangar molded into a cliff edge.

They could still hear the reverberations of the Snowman's maddened howl.

As the storm subsided, Bradford noticed the blackened ice being raised. The tissue embedded in the ice was giving off tremendous heat, fissuring the mountain, cutting a livid scar into the granite layers below the ice; flames burst through the ice. Fumaroles which heated the hot springs released sprays of acid-charged boiling water. Hummocks of black basalt leaped into the air from the underground gas jets. The ice below them dissolved into a bubbling white-hot bed of lava which gashed the mountain, then descended to the lower slopes.

Bradford staggered back and crouched against the wall with Spider.

"Where's Pemba?"

"He says the weather's getting worse. He's gone ahead to look for shelter. If we stay here we'll freeze to death," Spider replied with resignation.

Bradford groped for his thermometer and altimeter. They were just under eighteen thousand feet; the temperature had dropped to forty below zero. He could see the clouds at the summit, driven by the wind. The storm was gaining power; by late afternoon it would be a full-scale blizzard. He saw sheets of snow flung up from the névé, the source snowfield at the terminus of the glacier. They were trapped between currents of air from above and below; the storm would envelop them if they stayed where they were.

Bradford wondered now whether he actually cared about living or dying on the mountain. Would it really matter? He felt lost and confused. Jamie's death had shocked him, made him relive the scene on Lhotse. If Packard was also gone, the three of them would surely be claimed by the mountain. His mind focused on the word "Sierra." A chain of mountains with serrated edges. Yes, they were like sharpened, blazing knives raised against him.

It would be better if the mountain took him, he told

himself, because he could not live with the thought of failing again. He had come after the Snowman this time to reclaim that part of him which had died. Now he no longer had the strength. He slumped onto his side, opening his arms, waiting for the blizzard to embrace him, to relieve him of the agony of confronting the Snowman another time.

On the other side of the sangar he saw a fleck of orange. It gradually grew larger, until he realized that it was Pemba. He had girdled the cirque below the summit. He moved agilely along the circle of cliffs contorted by the glacier.

Bradford's eyes were closed when he heard the voice.

"Thik hai?" the voice called out.

Was he all right? What a question.

He was shaken, then yanked to his feet.

"Dan, you've got to move."

Pemba brushed the snow off his suit, then adjusted the mixture on Spider's oxygen nozzle to enrich the flow.

"I found a cave beyond the cirque."

Bradford's legs wobbled, and he supported himself on the sangar wall.

"Where are the Dexedrine tablets?" Pemba asked.

Bradford indicated his pack; the Sherpa stuck his hand inside and found the medical bag. He broke out the tablets, swallowed one without water, and then undid Spider's oxygen mask and forced one down Spider's throat along with some new snow. Spider reeled drunkenly without the oxygen. His mouth hung open, and he was almost overcome by anoxia. Still weak and despondent, Bradford helped Pemba replace the mask. Spider began to breathe too rapidly.

"Slow down," Pemba ordered him. "Try to keep your breathing in a rhythm."

With Pemba at the head belaying them with the rope, they gradually circled an outlier which had been concealed by the storm. The minor peak extending out beyond the principal summit enabled them to climb in a traverse so that they could avoid the main path of the storm.

When Bradford looked back, the sangar they had left was no longer visible. A blanket of snow cloaked it, and gale-force winds lashed it unremittingly. They had moved south of the summit. The route to the top would not go, for the sheer face collapsed into an acute angle of perhaps twenty degrees. If they were to make an assault they would have to retrace the same path, and in these weather conditions it would be impossible.

Pemba seemed to glide along the depression of granite ice. When he finally stopped, they were just above a long, undulating couloir which had been formed when the glacier changed direction. Twisted spears of ice grew out of the mountainside like thorns, concealing the entrance to the cave. But mountains held no mysteries for Pemba. He deciphered signs which a mountain concealed from strangers.

They shone their flashlights into the mouth of the cave. It was like entering a frozen womb which contained the secrets of the earth's birth. The cave had been limestone when the mountain was a seething volcanic mass, spewing forth gases and molten lava. From its roof icicle-tortured masses of multicolored stalactites hung, like a cripple's contorted fingers. Growing up from the cavern floor, stalagmites joined them, creating a bizzare convoluted shape. Where the two met, solid pillars of ice were established. Spider was more frightened and tentative than he had been on the mountain; he shied away from the entrance.

"It isn't safe," he protested. The horns of ice were ominous and beautiful, suggesting a primeval temple of worship, at once inscrutable and forbidden. "I'm not going in."

"Okay with me," Bradford said, his voice echoing like a church bell.

Pemba and Bradford worked their way into the belly of the cave. Where it widened there was ample room to set up the primus and stretch out in comfort. Pemba lit the stove, then unwrapped the provisions he carried in his pack. He threw salt pork and thick strips of bacon into a frypan, adding beans and frozen potatoes.

Spider inched his way toward them as though spying on his enemies.

The bacon crackled in the frypan, sending up shafts of warm smoke which teased their noses. Soon Spider was crouched over the frypan. "What if there's another avalanche and we're sealed in here?" he asked.

"We hadn't considered the possibility," Bradford replied. "When I was a Boy Scout I learned that it was a fucking good idea to get inside—anywhere—when my ass was getting wet."

"But what if the Snowman finds us here?" he insisted.

"We'll be killed," Pemba observed.

"I got claustrophobia," Spider said, staring at the colored burrs of ice which hung on the stalactites like a pattern of knobs.

"Spider, you've got problems."

The bacon crisped and the ragout was dexterously dished out by Pemba on the aluminum mess plates.

Spider still balked, and circled them nervously. "Have you got a damned thing to say about Jamie?"

Bradford placed his spoon on the edge of his plate. "We tried to save him, didn't we? It could have been any of us. We've still got to eat. Now stop behaving like a righteous asshole. This is called survival. Right now it's the three of us against the Snowman. The odds stink, the weather's a son of a bitch, and griping isn't going to solve our problems."

"Do you think you could've killed him?" Spider asked, helping himself to a plate of steaming food.

"I wouldn't count on it," Bradford said. "When you wound a lion he becomes more dangerous."

"That's reassuring—we're never going to get down alive."

Chapter Twenty

Spider insisted on taking the first watch. The cave gave him the horrors, so he sat vigilantly at the mouth, muttering to himself, while the other two slept inside. His frustration grew more intense as the minutes ticked by.

The night was clear; he felt that he could almost touch the stars. He was absolutely convinced that if he could establish some communication link, Monte Dale would send up a chopper to rescue them. He'd seen choppers land on a pinpoint in Laos on terrain that was as impassable as this mountain. All they needed was a few hours of good weather. Monte and the authorities must be deeply concerned about the team; once they had a fix on the climbers' position they would mount an evacuation operation. But how could they even begin to plan a rescue if they couldn't locate them?

Spider left the cave, convinced that his mission was to lead them all to safety. A windbreak wall diverted the heavy, crashing winds; for the first time in days he felt secure. He flashed his light around to be sure that the footing was secure. A flat ice platform extended beyond the cave, and Spider circumspectly walked along it. He stopped when he heard muted shouts and strangled cries coming from below. There was a girl's nerve-rending helpless wail, followed by a boy's pathetic whine. Then he could've sworn he heard the Kodiak's agonized roar resounding through the enclosed valley adjacent to the cave. It couldn't be the wind. The sounds were too distinct and well defined to be gusts of air trapped in a chimney.

The mountain was alive with trapped, wounded people, pleading for assistance. He'd been right to come out and investigate.

He took out his flare gun and fired a flare. There was a dull report, and the sky was lighted with a majestic flash of red-orange, which comforted him. The cries rang out again, and he shouted, "Hang on, they'll be coming up for us!"

The thought virtually guaranteed the act, and he congratulated himself for taking the lead. Bradford was insane and the Sherpa was too ignorant to understand the meaning of life. They were savages. The flare died. He fired another one, then another, and the sky was turned into a small man-made galaxy of light. Of them all, Spider knew that he was behaving with true courage —heroically. He waited for more responses from the trapped people, and when the new flares sputtered, he reloaded his gun, poised and expectant.

"Don't give up. I'm with you," he called out to give them fortitude. "You're not alone."

The wound was so piercing that for a moment he wasn't aware of it. But the warm, gushing blood began to spurt, and when he covered it with his gloved hand he realized that he had a hole in his side. His legs became numb and the stars appeared to move on a reckless collision course, like planes in a midair crash.

He reeled dizzily, expecting to fall to the ground, but he was lifted up, defying gravity. The stab wounds were becoming more frequent, and he was being forced into a cave in which sparks flew as though from a blacksmith's anvil.

The cries of the girl and the child and the bear were mingled with his own, and the cave became a massive bed of gnashing spikes which gave off the intense heat of a blast furnace, searing his skin. Teeth dug into his face.

Dark patches of frozen blood laminated the snow outside the cave. Pemba held the flare gun in his hand and in a futile angry gesture flung it down the side of the mountain. He had tears in his eyes and strode toward Bradford, who looked impassively at the signs of death. Bradford embraced him; then, when Pemba had regained his calm, he pointed upward.

"We're going for the summit. It's our only chance."

The mountain was an unbroken white cataract. The earth that existed for the two of them was an unyielding ocean of filmy ice. The silence was intolerable, a deadly pall of frost which enveloped them, slowly crushing the life out of them.

"Spider panicked," Bradford said regretfully. "The cave spooked him."

"Dan, let's head down. We can double the ropes and rappel." Pemba looked at him hopefully. His breath was crystallized by the brutal cold. The summit with its treacherous ice towers loomed above them in clear outline. At the source of the glacier the snow had hardened to firn. The granules were as sharp as broken glass. Ridges of snow, sastrugi, as impenetrable as concrete, had been built up by the virulent winds.

Pemba's body shrieked with the agony of the cold. He had known such a sensation only when he crossed the Geneva Spur from Nuptse in the Himalayas and a freak storm had dropped the temperature to fifty degrees below zero.

It seemed colder now.

"I'm going up," Bradford said with finality. "Alone if I have to."

Pemba shook his head ruefully and pressed his palms together.

"I won't leave you. We should have died on Lhotse with the others. God gave us ten years and our destiny is the same."

"I don't want to die."

Pemba laughed. "We have no choice."

They climbed methodically across the terminus of the glacier. It was too cold to use the conventional prusik knots on the ascent; they switched to Jumar ascenders, mechanical clamping devices that enabled them to push up. The cam gripping the rope had a mouth of blunted teeth to prevent slippage. If there was any upward motion of rope beyond the cam, the Jumar would automatically grip the rope and prevent it from sliding.

At its most precipitous point the great façade of the glacier revealed white granite rock that appeared to be translucent, volcanic glass formed hundreds of thousands of years before. It was overlaid with a darker sedimentary rock border that looked like a massive wound that had hemorrhaged. A rock needle hung precariously from the slope. They were climbing on a forty-five degree angle. If any of the steel pitons holding the rope loosened, they would both fall into the enormous cwm below them. The enclosed valley at the foot of the glacier was some eight thousand feet below them. A drop from this height would last an eternity of four minutes.

It began to snow; wave-shaped masses of firn blasted in their faces. Exhausted, they stopped some two hundred feet below the summit and clung to the mountain like monkeys. A sudden thunderous crash of ice blocks shook the mountain, sending slopes of stones tumbling down.

Through the veil of snow, the Snowman appeared. He swung his single arm like an ax, hacking through the glacier. The ground under the men rumbled.

The speed at which the Snowman moved was alarming. He thrashed at the ice face in a frenzy, dislodging the pitons they had hammered in, cutting them off from their route down. Bradford hugged the flank of ice and set himself in firing position. The Snowman was coming into range.

Bradford scraped the ice from the telescopic sight with his teeth; it was still too heavily caked to see through. His fingers were numb; he threshed them hard against his side to regain some feeling.

"Pemba, fire, damn it, fire!" he implored.

Pemba stood transfixed, frozen with shock. He fell to his knees, shuddering.

Relentlessly the Snowman carved out a path on the sheer incline. Now he was only twenty yards away. His head was the size of a boulder. His breath hissed, searing the ice. Bradford's fingers twitched, and with his little finger he managed to release the automatic trigger.

The arrow lodged in the Snowman's side. A squall

of whining, bleating, tormented, incoherent sounds scattered from the monster's throat. Half of the massive body was demolished, and he fell backward, crashing onto the icefall.

The ice below Bradford was smoking, blackened by fire. The ridge became a bed of smoldering purple-red lava. The slopes below were fissuring; masses of granite ice were dropping into the enclosed valley.

Bradford struck Pemba across the face with his gloved hand; the blow shook the Sherpa out of his state of shock. He began climbing again toward the summit, followed by Bradford. When they reached the top, the storm ceiling had dropped; they could see the mountain boring open as though it had been bombed. It had become totally unstable. Huge séracs were ripped off, tumbling down thousands of feet. Sections of the glacier were penetrated so deeply that underground springs fed by boiling gases escaped, sending geysers of smoking water straight up in the air.

"We've done it. He's dead," Bradford whispered in awe.

But the Snowman had destroyed them in the process. We're alive but we're trapped, Bradford told himself. One canceled out the other. Radio communication was impossible from that altitude. He and Pemba lay prone, unable to move. The cutting boreal cold made them listless. They knew that unless a rescue helicopter had been sent out they would freeze to death, but they could not help themselves.

Cut off from both camps, with most of their provisions gone, there was no way for them but the northern slopes; yet arctic winds from that direction would tangle their ropes. They could not climb. Even standing was an effort. The cold had captured them. They would die its prisoners.

He roused Pemba, and the two of them struggled to a crested eave of ice, which shielded them from the corruscating sunlight. They built a small fire and huddled against the ice wall. Beneath them the scarred belly of the mountain still emitted noises of protest.

Under the frozen slush of the glacier which had shattered at the terminus, a piercing light flashed intermittently. Digging deep in the jungle expanse of underground ice, the Snowman writhed in agony. His claws raked over the rock covered with feldspar crystals. He battered down dense walls of ice and worked the throbbing mass of nerve ends against the fallen ice to relieve the horrible burning sensation.

Some preconscious memory of survival informed the effort. He whined shrilly in these opaque caverns under the ,surface. The sounds oscillated, carrying through the twisted angles of the glacier and fragmented weak sections which burst through the ground, altering its course. Pumice showered from black obsidian domes and was flung into the air, and the effect from the helicopter circling the mountain was of some cataclysmic malevolent force of nature that had erupted from the bowels of the earth.

Chapter Twenty-One

Ashby searched the mountain with binoculars from the helicopter, then handed them to Cathy. The deep pockets under his eyes and the nervous tic below his heart revealed the unbearable strain of the three-day search for Bradford and his men. There was no sign of them. Camp One had vanished. The second camp had been ravaged. They had been swallowed up by the mountain, and Ashby knew that he was to blame. If he had acted responsibly, confided in Garson and brought in the National Guard at the beginning, the slaughter which had occurred on the mountain need never have happened. Two more people had died that morning. His ambition had seemed to him innocent, but had made a mass murderer of him.

What had possessed him to hide the truth? Had the years of frustration, the routine of bringing out a weekly paper for a small community that seemed indifferent, forged him into the instrument of tragedy? There were no answers, and what made matters worse was that legally he could not be convicted of any crime.

He would have to live in Sierra under the cold scrutiny of his former friends. Word would get around about his part, and the locals would pull their advertising, cancel their subscriptions. If only he could be out on the mountain under the ice with Bradford. He envied Bradford his hero's death.

Cathy, beside him, put down the glasses. She moved away from the window, determined not to cry. It would be useless.

Chuck reported to the three Army helicopters that he was going to make a final sortie around the summit, then come in. Sheriff Garson glared at Monte and Ashby.

"Well, you got your way up to now. But I've made a few hard decisions, and I don't give two shits how I look. When we get down, I'm calling a press conference, and I plan to spill my guts. Sure, I'll seem a dummy to a lot of people, but at least I'll be able to live with myself."

His words bounced off Cathy's ears. Bradford was lost. The sky was a pellucid blue; if there was any sign of them they would have been spotted by now.

The chopper jumped wildly in air pockets, shaking them. The pilot turned apologetically and said, "Last look."

"Cover the northern slopes before you call it a day," Monte said.

Garson looked away from the window.

"It's unbelievable—the mountain's exploding." He pointed out the window. "Do you see that light down there, Cathy?"

She held up the glasses and studied the ground for a moment.

214

"It's the sun reflecting," she said, unwilling to give herself false hope.

"Nope. It's moving."

The pilot peered out and said he would follow it.

"Could they be trapped underground?" Monte asked.

"I doubt it," Garson replied. "My guess is they were killed in the avalanche."

The light changed colors, forming a rainbow in the ice matrix. What puzzled them was the way the area of light was concentrated, and its sudden, unpredictable motion. It changed direction inexplicably, bending across gulleys before resuming an upward, easterly path. The sun had already moved to the west. The source of light was coming from something else.

The chopper climbed over a large cascade of peaks some distance below the summit. The rainbow traveled relentlessly. Cathy felt herself shiver. She did not want to begin to hope again.

He's gone, she repeated to herself, and I've got to stop believing that there might be a chance that he's still alive. She gripped her seat belt hard, until her fingers were numb.

At the summit, Bradford gnawed at soda crackers like a starving rat. Pemba had gained control of himself, was exploring the summit, refusing now to accept their predicament. They still had their ice axes, rope, and enough pitons so that they could climb the difficult ice pitches belayed to the rope.

"Dan, there's something out there!" he shouted, standing at the ledge of precipice. Bradford pretended he did not hear and curled farther into the wall, hugging it. "Dan!"

Bradford finally roused himself and staggered to his

feet. He was very tired. The cold had lacerated his face raw, and the wounds were deep and scaly. He would wait until dark, then share the sleeping pills with Pemba.

He would die like a philosopher, proudly and without regrets. He would yield, and that would be his ultimate victory. A holistic welding together of body and spirit.

The enormous frozen void of the mountain embraced him, and he welcomed it like a lover.

"Do you see that?" Pemba pointed to the rainbow lighting the glazed torn ice of the slopes.

"It's light refraction," he said, surveying the great barren expanse, the connoisseur of death. And yet he wasn't satisfied with the facile explanation. Light did not move in this manner. "A storm's building. Put on your goggles or you'll go snowblind," he added, as though such considerations were still relevant. The image of himself foundering on the mountain, crying for help, offended him. Sheets of snow flew dervishly on the summit now.

"It's coming closer," he said as the definition of the rainbow sharpened. He could not ignore the tumultuous violent rumble of ice shifting and being crushed underneath the rib of rock running down from the main ridge. The spur was as slender as a woman's ankle, and it shook from pressure coming from within it.

It broke like glass. Slivers of it tumbled down onto a bergschrund which was also beginning to fracture. The summit itself was becoming unstable; ice boulders collapsed, forming a narrow shelf.

The Snowman's clawed hand broke through the ice crust below, and he began to climb on the surface to the summit. His mutilated torso stained the snow a greenish-black color.

Pemba brought out his two arrows. Bradford took one from him, and they retreated to the ice wall.

The head of the Snowman with its protruding horns was visible, and the light from the eyes blinded them. The great jaws snapped open, and the rows of teeth ground together furiously, throwing off white-hot sparks. How could he still be alive? Bradford was dazed by the shock of it.

The Snowman moaned aberrantly, wounded and crazed with fury. Slithering to the shelf, he pawed the ground with his single arm.

Bradford stripped off his gloves and bit into his fingers like a wild animal himself, to keep the circulation going. He loaded the crossbow. The heavy, frozen telescopic sight was weighting it, and he broke it off.

"Shoot for the chest!" he shouted to Pemba, who was behind him.

"Sogpa! Sogpa!" Pemba screeched angrily.

The Snowman's hand probed the ground, dislodging a rim of ice on the shelf of the summit. Gusts of snow obscured him from time to time. Bradford played him like a giant marlin who had taken the bait. He drew the Snowman closer to him. The Snowman's movements were slow. Bradford knew that his only chance was to gamble on a head shot. The Snowman slithered on the shelf, then forced himself to his feet. All around him the snow was filled with black mucus dripping from his wounds.

Erect, he towered over the summit, an otherworldly colossus that had survived for millions of years and traveled halfway around the world to encounter its final destiny. He was majestic in his primitive ferocity, roaring like some ancient god for its sacrifices. The grotesque arm swung out like a lance in a desperate effort to locate its tormentors.

"The cable's frozen!" Pemba cried as he pressed the trigger device.

The Snowman closed in, and the ground rumbled as he strode forward, his feet battering the loose snow and flinging it up, creating a whiteout, so that he was visible for only an instant. Bradford stood motionless, his torn, bleeding finger gripping the automatic trigger. The light from the eyes was diffuse, spinning, flashing motes. The monster was perhaps ten yards away. The Snowman's breath came in heavy waves, and the air became fetid. The heat from the enormous mouth was intense.

Bradford caught sight of the large saucer-shaped eyes. He released the trigger of the crossbow, then lurched back, falling on a sharply-grained mound of ice.

The arrow struck the head, and it exploded, throwing up particles of ice and tissue which blackened the air. The stench was nauseating. Bradford choked with dry heaves. He crawled on all fours to the precipice.

The Snowman was still falling. Below him Bradford could see in the new configuration of the mountain a crevasse so broad and deep that it was impossible to judge where it bottomed out. It was a tortuous maze which extended across the breadth of the icefall.

He dropped his crossbow and walked to the ice wall. Pemba was on his knees, chanting the hypnotic prayer of the lamas.

"Om Mane Padme Om . . ."

Bradford was losing all sensation in his fingers and

toes. His outer gloves were frozen rock-hard. He stooped to pick them up and carried them in his teeth to the dying fire.

Pemba came toward him, moving fluidly. He manipulated the fingers of Bradford's gloves until they softened and he was able to place them on Bradford's hands.

The guy ropes were tangled. They spent almost an hour straightening them. There was no way of climbing down until the ropes could be doubled to enable them to rappel themselves to the lower slopes.

The weather stayed clear. In the frozen wasteland the mountain looked like a diamond tiara. It was gorgeous, rugged, and Bradford accepted the fact that it would be their tomb.

They climbed sluggishly, Pemba taking the lead as they negotiated a pythonlike chimney which shrilly whined with trapped wind. They swayed back and forth, jostling like marionettes on a string. In the due-north wind, ice caked on the ropes. It was just a matter of time before one of them lost his grip. As they girdled a stark cornice, Bradford felt his body give out on him. He did not respond to Pemba's furious tugs on the rope.

"More slack!" Pemba shouted up to him.

Bradford shook his head and raised his hand, but he was too tired even to wave. The drop into a couloir guarding the north face was perhaps three thousand feet. He would black out the moment he became weightless, plunging in a free fall. He would extend his arms like a diver and float downward in an exquisite swan dive.

"Don't, Dan, Dan," Pemba implored him. "You'll take me with you."

Pemba was right. He would be killing his friend, for

219

no man could survive on the mountain alone. He held on to the rope and lowered himself to the pitch where Pemba waited. The tears in his eyes had frozen; elliptical icicles hung from his cheeks.

"I can't make it. We'll take the pills and it'll be over in less than an hour," Bradford said, pleading his case.

"You don't have the right to take my life from me. Only God can do that."

He did not have the energy to protest. When he slumped down, he felt Pemba's boot dig into his hip.

"Get up!"

He fought with his body, but his reflexes were going. The numbness spread over him. It was an odd sensation, dying in the clear bright sunlight. He had always imagined that it would be dark. Somehow the absence of light would make the last moments acceptable.

The sky was separating into two warlike camps. To the east patches of slate cloud carried a storm, and to the west there were ghostly intimations of a summer's day. In the distance they heard a sound and looked up. The sound was moving closer, insistent and defiant. A helicopter's rotors carried in the wind like the whine of a mosquito on a warm night. The helicopter climbed over the icefall.

Pemba began to wave his arms frantically and shout at the top of his voice. The rotors churned, and the sound moved perceptibly closer. It circled, then closed above them. Bradford slammed his ax into the wall of ice, anchoring it. He lifted himself to his feet and feebly turned his head as the chopper flashed a Morse signal to them.

He urged his body to respond, lifted his arm, and waved. He had survived and vindicated himself. The lamas who had saved him before would eventually learn that the Snowman was dead and be released from their bondage. As he looked down the side of the mountain, there was a huge black shadow outlined in the ice.

IT BEGAN WITH JUST AN ORDINARY LITTLE DOG.

RABID

by David Anne

John and Paula had thought they had found the perfect way to end their holiday in France. They had had fun outwitting the authorities by smuggling a dog into England. And Asp was a beautiful, loving corgi with soft fur and limpid eyes. But the horrible virus she concealed paralyzed first a town, then the nation with fear. As the disease mutated and became airbone, it lashed out to terrorize the entire world!

A DELL BOOK $1.95